A Forbidden Love

White Owl turned slowly around to face her again. "I do not know this man—your father, but I have known enough white men to know that he will never understand why we are together."

"Together?" Rose asked. "Are we—together?"

He took one of her hands—it seemed so small and fragile in his own large, rough hand. Her porcelain skin looked even paler against his. "Ever since I first laid eyes on you, I knew that I had to make you my woman. It was a feeling that was stronger than anything I have ever known before, and I am a man who goes after what he wants." He pulled her close to him and let his gaze meet hers, as he added, "And, my Wild Rose, I want you."

D1518445

Other *Leisure* books by Veronica Blake:

BLACK HORSE

VERONICA BLAKE

WHITE OWL

Dorchester
Publishing

DORCHESTER PUBLISHING

January 2011

Published by

Dorchester Publishing Co., Inc.
200 Madison Avenue
New York, NY 10016

ISBN 13: 978-1-4285-1133-0
E-ISBN: 978-1-4285-0914-6

The "DP" logo is the property of Dorchester Publishing Co., Inc.

Printed in the United States of America.

Visit us online at www.dorchesterpub.com.

Having another book published by Dorchester Publishing is definitely a dream come true, and I would like to thank my wonderful editor, Leah Hultenschmidt, for making this become a reality.

I would also like to thank my friend, Lynne Zydonik, for her friendship and encouragement.

A very special thank-you, as always, to my amazing family for their constant support and understanding.

WHITE OWL

To Susan!
Thank You,

Veronica
Blake

9/10/2011

Chapter One

Owl scanned the ridgeline for the woman. He had seen her on top of the plateau every day for more than a week. If she showed up today, he planned to get a closer look and perhaps ask her what she found so fascinating about the Utes' afternoon activities.

In the meadow below, White Owl's comrades were partaking in their favorite pastime. The track they had worn into the ground to race their ponies on was one of the best they had ever had, and there was no greater joy than competing with one another for the chance to be known as the Ute brave with the fastest pony.

For the past several days, however, White Owl's attention had been diverted from the races by the woman who hid in the bushes and watched them.

The loud hooting and hollering of his comrades combined with the pounding of horse hooves against the hard ground nearly drowned out the sound of the approaching horse. It wasn't until she was already in her hiding spot that White Owl realized the woman was here. From his viewpoint he could barely see the dark brown tip of her horse's nose sticking out from the bushes. He could not see anything of the woman. But it would only be a matter of minutes before the two horses spotted each other.

With a swift kick in his horse's sides, White Owl and his horse lunged forward and in a couple of strides were directly in front of the woman and her pony. He pulled hard on the reins and brought his horse to an abrupt halt while the other horse snorted and tossed its head in surprise. His gaze was drawn to the woman's eyes . . . they were as blue as the midday sky overhead.

Although it had only been his intention to let the woman know he was aware that she was watching them race their ponies, it was White Owl who was caught off guard. The constricted feeling in his throat made speaking impossible, and his heart felt as if it was about to pound out of his chest. It seemed as though they stared at one another forever before White Owl was finally able to gain control of his senses. Then, he did the only thing that he could think of doing at this awkward moment—he gave the woman a sly smile and eyed her entire body in an obvious appraisal. With a toss of his head that sent his long raven hair swirling back over his bare shoulders, White Owl spun his horse around and with a gleeful war whoop galloped back down the hillside in a cloud of dirt and rocks.

Rosaline Adair stared at the swirl of dust that rose in front of her face as if she was in a trance. The Ute's unexpected appearance had left her without one coherent thought. Once her shock began to fade, her father's heavily accented Irish voice raced through her head, "Don't ride out alone. Them Indians will snatch you up quicker than the blink of an eye, and that will be the end of you, Rosie girl."

She was certain that she had just stared her "end" right in the face. He was even more terrifying since she had never been so close to a Ute warrior before. At the nearby White River Indian Agency, she had only seen Indian women and children, and occasionally one of the older Ute chiefs. The younger Ute men did not like anything that was associated with the agency or with the homesteaders who were moving in on all the surrounding lands.

Rose pressed her hand against her chest and attempted to take a full breath. The dust the Indian's horse had stirred up made her cough and caused her eyes to sting, but she didn't take the time to wipe the dirt from her bleary gaze. She had to get out of here now. Her obedient mare, Molly, seemed to sense her fear as they hurried down the back side of the slope. Once they were on flat ground, she kicked the horse in the sides, and the animal lunged forward in a gallop that matched the thudding of Rose's frantic heartbeat.

Although there was no sign the Indian was following her, Rose's panic continued to increase until she was within sight of the house where she lived with her parents and two brothers.

Rose slowed Molly to a trot. She took a couple more deep breaths in an attempt to calm down as she approached the corral where her father and younger brother, Donavan, were busy filling the horse troughs with water. She yanked down the wide brim of her brown hat in an effort to hide as much of her face as possible when she rode past them.

"Hey, Sis," Donavan called out. "Where you been?"

Rose waved and forced a weak smile as she rode by, but she did not attempt to speak. She could not trust her voice since her entire body was still shaking from her brief encounter with the Ute brave. When her father glanced up at her, Rose avoided meeting his gaze and continued to ride toward their newly built barn. Her smile faded the instant she was inside. As she slid from Molly's back a loud voice rang out. She closed her eyes tightly and tried to prepare herself for the accusations she knew would come.

"You look mighty guilty. What have you been up to?"

Rose turned slowly to face Tate, her twin brother. "W-what do you m-mean? I was just riding Molly down by the creek." She shrugged her shoulders in a nonchalant manner. "I sat on the creek bed for a spell and enjoyed this wonderful weather we are having." She could tell that he was not in the mood for friendly chitchat.

"Well, there are plenty of chores to be done, and you're out gallivantin' around. Besides, remember what Pa told you about them Injuns."

"I know what Pa said," Rose retorted with an indignant toss of her head as she led her horse into her stall. She undid the cinch and pulled the saddle from Molly's back, then hoisted it over the rail as she fought the urge to engage in another battle with her brother.

"That horse looks like she's been run a lot farther than from just down by the creek." Tate shook his head and added, "You'd best go see if Ma needs help and quit actin' like you're some princess who doesn't need to work. I'll finish takin' care of Molly."

Rose clenched her teeth together until they hurt. She had the same rich red hair color as her brother and a similar shade of blue eyes, but beyond those physical traits, there was nothing else they had in common. Tate was a copy of their father. Both were unyielding and opinionated to the point that it was impossible to reason with them most of the time. Rose sighed heavily. "I'm on my way to help Ma right now. Thanks for tending to Molly."

She stomped past her twin without glancing in his direction or giving him a chance to say anything else. Once out of the barn, Rose practically ran to the house. She could fib to Tate, but if her father confronted her about her whereabouts, she would have a hard time lying to him. Once she was in the house and realized that her mother was nowhere in sight, she sighed with relief. She was definitely not ready to face her mother.

Like the barn, the home that she shared with her parents and brothers was recently finished. The sprawling log cabin consisted of one large room that housed the kitchen, living and dining area;

three small rooms provided one bedroom for her parents, one shared by her brothers and, thankfully, one for Rose to occupy alone. She rushed to her little sanctuary now and closed the heavy woolen curtain before tossing her hat on the bureau and throwing herself down on her bed face-first.

What had she been thinking? She knew riding so far from home was dangerous, and she definitely should not have been on Ute land. The Northern Utes, or *Noochew* Utes, who lived in the mountains and plains in the nearby villages barely tolerated the whites homesteading in the surrounding areas. But lately the tension was drawn tighter each day between the Indians and the whites—thanks to Nathan Meeker, the Indian agent at the White River Indian Agency.

Rose rolled over on her back and stared up at the roughly hewn log ceiling. The Ute's image swam before her eyes. She clasped her hand over her mouth to keep from crying out. Had it just been an accidental encounter, or had he known that she was up on that plateau?

She had come upon the games by accident one afternoon when she had gone farther than she realized on one of her daily rides. As she had crested the ridge of a small hill, she heard loud whooping and the thunderous roar of pounding hooves. Thinking that she was about to be attacked, Rose had hidden herself and Molly in a large clump of thick aspens and bushes on top of the hill. Much to her relief, and then to her delight, Rose realized that she had just discovered the Utes' horse races.

The races were one of the most exciting things she had ever seen, and for over a week, she had been sneaking back to the hilltop to watch the fun and games. Until today, she had thought she had a good hiding spot.

The Ute warrior dominated Rose's thoughts again in spite of her best efforts to wipe out his memory. The brazen way his dark eyes had traipsed over her body made it obvious that he knew he could take anything from her that he wanted. A violent tremor shook through her.

"There you are. I was gettin' worried about you. These rides of yours are getting longer and longer, and you know that you have to be careful out there," Rose's mother said as she entered her daughter's room.

Rose quickly jumped up from her bed but had to grasp the edge of the dresser that sat beside her bed to steady herself. "I—I know, and I intend to stay closer to home from now on." As soon as the words fell from her mouth, Rose knew that she had said more than she should have. The look of alarm on her mother's face was undeniable.

"Why? Did something happen to you when you were out riding? Those Indians—"

"Oh no, nothing happened," Rose interrupted. "Nothing at all. It's just that I realize how selfish I've been lately—riding Molly so much when I should be here helping you out."

"Rosaline—it's your ma you're talkin' to." Colleen Adair shook her finger at her daughter as she added, "And I can tell by the look on your face that you're lyin' to me. But all that matters now is that you're safe. And with the grace of the Lord above, I hope you learned yourself a lesson by whatever it was that scared you so bad today." Turning around to head out of the door, she added, "It's almost time to start dinner, so I'll take you up on that offer for help."

Rose gave a weak nod as her mother looked back over her shoulder and said, "You do not have a selfish bone in your body, Rosie, but even a little white lie can sometimes be a person's downfall."

"Sorry," Rose mumbled. A feeling of shame washed over her. Her mother was definitely right about one thing; she had learned a huge lesson today.

She shook her head and threw her hands over her eyes. But the Ute's image was still there—smiling that wicked smile and looking at her as if he had no decency at all. She ran the back of her hand across her forehead to wipe away the perspiration suddenly on her brow.

Well, it would be the last time he looked at her in that manner, Rose swore to herself, because she would never stray over to Ute land again.

Chapter Two

White Owl sat cross-legged at the fire pit in front of his tepee and watched the flames dancing among the logs. He expelled a heavy sigh and frowned. He had thought of nothing but the girl with hair the color of a fiery sunset and eyes as blue as the mountain lakes since he had seen her on the plateau earlier today. He tried to focus on the fire, but he could not rid himself of her memory.

"What has my first son so angry?"

White Owl shook his head in an aggravated manner and glanced up at his father. Strong Elk smiled down at him and crossed his arms over his broad chest as he waited for an answer.

White Owl shrugged as he returned his gaze to the fire. "A woman," he answered.

Strong Elk chuckled as he sat on the ground next to his eldest son. "Is it Sunshine? I've seen how she watches you. Her hips are wide for bearing your sons. She will be a good wife."

White Owl scowled but did not immediately reply. If only Sunshine made him feel the way the white girl did today, then there would not be a problem.

"It is another girl?" Strong Elk asked. His thick dark brows lifted up in surprise. "Well, you can have more than one wife, so you could have Sunshine and . . ." He left the question hanging as he waited for his son to reply.

With a grunt, White Owl threw a rock into the fire. "She is not *Uncompahgre*."

Strong Elk chuckled again and smacked his son on the back. "Is she from the Yampah tribe? It would be good to have a wife from that tribe. They are very spiritual and strong."

"She is not *Yuuttaa*, father. She is white."

The following silence told White Owl that his father was stunned to hear that the woman his son was thinking about was not Ute.

"How is it that you have encountered this white woman?" Strong Elk finally asked.

"She has been coming to watch the pony races. I noticed her on the plateau and went up to get a closer look." White Owl shook his head and gave a defeated sigh.

"And with just a look this woman is doing this to you, or did something else happen?"

White Owl shook his head again as he met his father's worried gaze. "I did not do something foolish, if that is what you mean." He glanced away and added, "But I might if I see her again. She has stolen my mind. I cannot think of anything but her."

The sun slipped below the last horizon and the glow from the fire was the only light left on this night of a new *muatagoci*—"moon." White Owl could no longer see his father's expression clearly, but he heard him exhale sharply.

"There is trouble brewing at the agency already. We should not do anything that would cause the problems to get worse." Strong Elk rose up to his feet, then leaned down and rested his hand on his son's shoulder. "I do not worry about you, my son. You have never done crazy things that would disgrace me." He straightened up and added, "Not like your brother." A heavy sigh emitted from Strong Elk. "You can ponder this important matter during the Sun Dance. Until then I will pray to the bear to give you the strength to stay away from this woman."

White Owl nodded and smiled. "Thank you, Father." He watched him disappear into the darkness as he headed toward the tepee he shared with his wives, White Owl's mother, Sage, and also her younger sister, Cloud Woman. His father's words echoed through his mind. For his people— the *Yuuttaa*, or Ute, meaning "land of the sun"— the bear was considered a close and sacred relative. White Owl knew the bear had helped him to become the strong warrior that he was today . . . he just hoped the sacred bear would give him the wisdom to make the right decision where the white woman was concerned.

If he could be patient, White Owl could also ask the Great Spirit for guidance. In a few days the Utes would begin preparation for the most significant ceremony of their people. The Sun Dance took place in midsummer and was an important spiritual journey between the participant and the Great Spirit. After the ceremony was finished, White Owl's medicine would be strong and he would see things more clearly. Unfortunately, White Owl was not a very patient man.

For the past three days he had been watching for her, but she had not showed up again—that is, until today. White Owl had hidden his pony in the bushes halfway up the hillside and walked up here every afternoon, waiting for her to return. He still could not explain why he was so obsessed with the flame-haired woman, but if she was worth missing out on the races with his comrades, she must be something special.

Watching her from the cover of the bushes now, White Owl was not sorry that he had chosen to wait for her instead of engaging in the games down below.

He had noticed her coming from the northeast, so she must have crossed Milk Creek. Obviously, she had ridden a long way to come here . . . perhaps she was as curious about him as he was about her.

From his hiding spot, he could see her clearly. The other day her hair had been in a tight bun at the nape of her neck, and she had worn the same brown wide-brimmed hat that she wore today. But now, with her long red hair flowing freely around her face, she was even more beautiful than White Owl remembered. Last time, she had been dressed in a simple black riding skirt, red plaid shirt, and looked like a homesteader's daughter. Now she wore a matching tan jacket and riding skirt that looked expensive. He was reminded of the rich women he had seen in Denver when he was young and had been sent there to learn the ways of the white man.

He suspected that she would not hide in the same location as she had a few days ago, and his prediction had been correct. Since she had ridden her horse to the far end of the hillside, he was only a few yards away from her. He was certain that she could not see him, but he could watch every move she made, and she seemed confident that she had found a good hiding spot as she removed her riding jacket and pushed it into her saddlebags. White Owl noticed she moved cautiously so that she would not draw any attention to herself. Fascinated, he watched her roll up the sleeves of her fancy white top and remove her brown hat for a moment to wipe the sweat from her brow with the tips of her fingers. The sun was scorching on this summer afternoon, and White Owl was hoping she would remove more clothing. He was disappointed when her attention seemed to focus on the pony races in the meadow below them.

Although he did not have a plan beyond waiting here in the bushes to see if the girl came back, White Owl now discovered that he was completely hypnotized by her. The bright afternoon sunlight glistened on her red hair and almost seemed to cast a mystical glow around her entire face. Her skin looked as creamy as milk and her eyes definitely were the most vibrant blue he had ever seen. He could do nothing other than stare at her.

When he finally began to snap out of the spell that this enchanting girl was casting over him, White Owl realized that he wanted to do far more than watch her from this hiding place. The willpower that he had prayed to the bear to give him when he encountered this woman again was completely forgotten.

He bounded up from the sagebrush that had been concealing him and lunged forward. He heard the girl's terrified cry and saw her horse rear up in surprise, but before she could get her horse under control again, White Owl grabbed her foot and pulled her down from the animal's back. They both tumbled to the ground, with White Owl landing first and the girl crashing down on top of him. For a moment, he could not catch his breath. But even as he gasped for air, he wrapped his arms tightly around his captive to keep her from getting away.

Although he was expecting a fight, White Owl was not prepared for the wildcat he had just captured. He felt her fingernails rake through the skin on his shoulder, but the pain from that attack was lost to the rest of the battle he encountered as her kicks at his legs and the punches of her fists against his chest and face took him completely by surprise.

Once White Owl was able to take a full breath, he regained his senses, along with his strength, and easily grasped the girl in a crushing embrace and rolled over with her until he was the one on top. He felt her body stiffen beneath him as she began to realize that he had her pinned so tightly between the ground and his body that she could not get away regardless of how hard she tried to fight him.

She finally gave up her intense struggle. White Owl could feel the rapid rising and falling of her breasts pressing against his bare chest as she attempted to breathe. The realization that only a bit of material prevented their skin from touching made his manhood rise without warning. The swollen member pushed unmercifully against her hip bone.

By the horrified look on her face, White Owl was certain that she was also aware of his desire. Her blue eyes went wide and her lips parted in a silent scream.

Her stunned silence lasted for only a moment before she started kicking and struggling against him with even more determination. White Owl was certain that her main target was his most private area, which was completely deflated now, because that was where her knees seemed to be aimed as she struggled beneath him again with renewed vigor. And though he had her arms pinned firmly against the ground with his hands, he could not get her flailing legs under control.

"Stop it, woman! I do not intend to hurt you."

Instantly, her struggles ceased. "You can speak English?"

"Not with pride—only because I did not know any better as a child when I was forced to learn the ways of your people."

She continued to stare up at him, but she did not attempt to fight him again. He could feel the heat of her rapid breath against his face. He could steal a kiss from those pale pink lips, and she would not be able to prevent it—a thought that made him swell with desire again.

"Oh, get off me now," the girl gasped as she began to kick violently again. "Get off!" she screamed even louder.

White Owl tried to put his hand over her mouth to silence her. There was no way he intended to share this beauty, and he had been lucky enough to avoid the other braves' questions about his whereabouts the past few afternoons. Once he released his tight grip on her arms, however, she began pounding her fists against his chest and his face as hard as she could. But at least she was no longer yelling.

Finally overpowering her once again, White Owl managed to pin her against the ground and put one hand over her mouth to muffle her protests. With as forceful a tone as he could evoke, he said, "You cannot scream or every one of those men down there will come, and they will not be as gentle as I am. Do you understand me?"

The girl stared at him for an instant, then slowly nodded. White Owl hoped he could trust her as he began to pull his hand away from her mouth. He reminded himself that he must control his sexual desires if he didn't want her screaming out in terror again. But the only way to do that was to remove himself from her luscious body right away.

He slid to the side and tried to keep his groin from touching any part of her. He did not release his tight hold on her arms until he was certain that she was not going to do anything rash. To his surprise, she remained unmoving and silent, but the frightened look on her face made her feelings toward him more than evident.

"I will not hurt you," White Owl said. "I only want to talk to you."

She did not reply and continued to stare at him as though she was about to pass out from fright.

"I've seen you up here. You like to watch the pony races." He gestured with a toss of his head toward the meadow down below.

He noticed her throat move when she swallowed; she wore a delicate gold chain with a little golden heart hanging from it. The sunlight reflecting from the necklace was almost blinding.

His attention was distracted from the shiny heart when she ran her tongue over her soft pink lips. White Owl was glad he was not still on top of her, because that one little swipe of her tongue sent his senses whirling and his manhood rising again.

"I do enjoy the races," she admitted.

White Owl nodded, thankful that she had not noticed the swell in his buckskin pants. "We have fun. It is rare that we can have fun now that the white man has invaded our lands."

The expression on the girl's face changed. She

did not appear to be quite as frightened of him, and it almost seemed as if she agreed with him when she nodded her head slightly.

"Where do you ride from?" he asked in an effort to change the subject. He decided to take a huge gamble and release her completely from his grip as he sat up. To his relief, she sat up, too, and made no effort to get away from him.

She stared at him for a moment before she answered. "It's a long way from here."

"I saw you ride in from the north, across Milk Creek." Her frightened look returned. He added, "I do not plan to hunt you or your family down, if that is your fear."

The girl continued to stare at him as if he had just guessed her exact thoughts. "I need to go now," she said in a choked voice.

"Will you come again?"

"No—I-I shouldn't, I can't."

"There is no reason for you to be afraid of me," he said. He noticed she glanced down at the other warriors around the racetrack.

She scooted a couple of inches away from him. "It would be wrong for us to meet here again."

White Owl leaned forward. "Why? Because I am not a white man?"

"No, of course not. It's just, well, my father, he has told me that I'm not allowed to ride out here alone anymore because of the trouble between the Utes and the people over at the Indian agency."

"Why are you here today then?" White Owl asked bluntly.

"Well, I . . . I just wanted to . . ." she started. "I'm not really sure why."

White Owl nodded, and a smug grin curved his mouth.

"Why are you looking at me like that?" she asked in a defensive tone. She inched a little farther away from him.

"Because I know why you are here—you came to see me again."

An indignant huff escaped from her. "It has nothing to do with you."

"What are you called?" he asked.

"Rosali—Rose, my name is Rose."

"Rose," White Owl repeated slowly. "Will you come back here tomorrow, Rose?"

The girl gave her head a negative shake, then slowly pushed herself up from the ground. White Owl followed her. Standing beside her, he realized that he was nearly a head taller than she was.

"I . . . no!" she retorted. Her gaze moved up to his face as if she was noticing how tall he was.

White Owl straightened his stance even more and puffed out his chest. He was sure she was impressed.

A blush colored her cheeks, and she quickly glanced away. She looked down at the racetrack again, then back at him. She shook her head as she added, "Coming here was a mistake. I—I cannot come back again."

White Owl watched with fascination as her shiny red curls swirled around her shoulders with the movement of her head. "I will come to see you then."

"No!" she gasped. "I thought you just said that you were not going to hunt for me or my family, and if you come to our ranch my father would kill you."

"Or I would kill him," White Owl retorted. He tilted his chin up in an arrogant manner.

The girl's blue gaze widened again, and White Owl could see how fearful she still was of him. He used this to his advantage. "I will see you here tomorrow then."

Without further comment, he turned around and went into the thick bushes. He went back down the incline to where he had hidden his pony. He smiled as he mounted.

Rose . . . with lips the same color as many of the delicate pink flowers that covered the hillsides and meadows. He would call her Wild Rose—his Wild Rose.

White Owl's smile widened. Tomorrow could not get here fast enough.

Chapter Three

"Oh my," Rose whispered as she crumpled back down to the ground. As desperately as she wanted to get away, there was no way her shaky legs were strong enough to carry her the short distance to where Molly stood waiting.

She swallowed the hard lump in the back of her throat. For three whole days she had been so good and fought the urge to go riding—even for a short distance. But today was such a perfect summer day. Not even the tiniest wisp of a cloud marred the vast expanse of blue overhead. Rose just had to go riding.

She had told her mother—and herself—that she was just going to ride Molly down by Milk Creek, which bordered her parents' property and served as an unofficial boundary line for the Ute lands. Once she had reached the creek, however, she had not even hesitated to nudge Molly into the gently flowing water. She had felt helpless to prevent herself from being drawn back to the Ute racetrack. Now look where it had gotten her!

Rose leaned forward cautiously and glanced through the bushes. She could see the Indian riding his black pony toward the racetrack. Had he been hiding up here every day for the past three days waiting to see if she would come back? She groaned and sat back down on her heels. How could she have been so stupid?

She looked down at her dirty and torn clothes and felt a tear sting the corner of her eye. The riding outfit and frilly white blouse she wore were her best suit of clothes and only a few of the store-bought garments she owned. Her Aunt Maggie had purchased them for her as a going-away present when they had left Denver to homestead out here in western Colorado over a year and a half ago. She knew it had been foolish to wear these nice clothes today, but for some reason she had felt compelled to dress up. Now her beautiful outfit was probably ruined.

In an effort to control the fierce tremors that continued to race through her body, Rose wrapped her arms tightly around herself. Somehow she had to gather her wits about her, get back home as quickly as possible, and pray that the Indian didn't follow through with his threat to come for her.

She peeked back through the bushes and could no longer see the Ute anywhere on the slope below. She hoped he had already rejoined the others and was now one of the many riders racing around the track in a veil of dust and rocks. Regardless of where he was, Rose knew she had to leave here now.

She reached out and picked up her wide-brimmed hat. It was covered with dust, and the top was flattened out of shape. With a couple of shakes, the loose dust was easily removed. She pushed the crown back into shape before she placed the hat back on her head.

Her shaky legs barely supported her as she made her way over to Molly. Her compliant mare had not moved one inch from where she had been standing when the Indian had pulled Rose from her back.

"Thank the good Lord above, Molly, that Pa trained you so good," Rose whispered as she led the horse away from the ridge and down the back side of the hill. Her legs still wobbled so much that she could barely stand up, let alone walk down the incline. Several times she slipped and slid a couple of feet down on her rear-end before she could regain her balance. Once they were on flat ground again, Rose attempted to climb back up into the saddle. Her arms felt as limp as a rag doll's, and it took all of her strength to pull herself onto Molly's back.

"Take me home, girl," Rose said with a trembling voice. The horse moved forward with cautious steps, as if she knew that her mistress was in a fragile state.

Rose continued to glance back over her shoulder even though she knew it was a wasted effort. If the Ute wanted to follow her, she would probably not even be aware of it until he was dragging her off her horse again. There were heavy groves of aspens and tall clusters of sagebrush and cedars scattered throughout the countryside. She had no doubt the Indian could easily track her all the way back to her parents' farm without ever showing himself. She shuddered and clasped the reins tighter as she urged Molly into a trot.

The trip back home seemed to take longer than normal because she could not stop berating herself for going to the racetrack. Even worse, she could not quit thinking about the feel of the Indian's rock-hard manhood against the side of her hip.

She suddenly had to undo the top button of her blouse, but that did nothing to cool the burning sensation that raced through her entire body. Since she had two brothers, Rose was not ignorant of male anatomy. When she and her twin brother had turned sixteen two years ago, her dear mother—in a whispered voice when no one was around—had told her a bit about what a woman was expected to do with a man once they married. But never had Rose imagined that a man could be that large and—and to think what he did to a woman with that—oh!

She wiped away the beads of sweat on her face. There was nothing she could do about the rivulets of perspiration that trailed between her breasts and down her body beneath her clothes.

What is wrong with me? she wondered. The memory of him should be so frightening that she needed to erase it from her mind completely. But rather than being scared stiff from the close call she had just had, her body seemed to act as if it had actually enjoyed the experience. Now, that was a terrifying thought.

In spite of herself, Rose turned around in her

saddle and looked behind her again. A sudden feeling of disappointment flooded through her. It was quickly followed by disgust and anger. There really must be something wrong with her. The Ute brave had as much as defiled her body and threatened to kill her father, yet she was still hoping to see him again?

"Lord forgive me," Rose cried out as she glanced up at the sky.

With Milk Creek far behind her, Rose let Molly's gallop slow to a steady trot. Although she attempted to convince herself that she should probably tell her father about the Ute's threat, she also knew that she would not say a word to him unless it became absolutely necessary. Paddy Adair's uncontrollable temper was something Rose preferred to avoid at all costs.

As she rode up to the barn, Rose was amazed that neither of her brothers or her father was anywhere to be seen. To her relief, she realized that they must still be working in the hay fields or out on the range checking on the cattle. The extra time was more than she could have hoped for because it gave her a chance to compose herself a bit before she had to face any of them. She took her time to wipe down Molly, water her, and give her an extra pitchfork of hay. She also gave the mare a half a bucket of oats—a real treat that the horse only got occasionally.

Once she had taken good care of her horse, Rose took a few more minutes to tidy herself up. She removed her hat and ran her fingers through her hair to untangle the long tendrils as best she could. Her riding skirt was dusty, but fortunately, there did not seem to be any tears. She brushed it off until there was not a trace of dust left. But her blouse was filthy and ripped in several places. She put her cropped jacket back on to cover up the tattered blouse. Would everything else that happened today be so easy to cover up?

"Well, there you be. I was comin' to check out in the barn to see if you were back yet. You were gone an awful long time again."

Rose clasped the front of her jacket tightly together with one hand and forced herself to smile at her mother when she met her at the front door stoop. "I've been out in the barn for a long time. I figured Molly deserved some extra grooming today."

Colleen's smile was genuine as she draped her arm over her daughter's shoulder and walked into the house with her. "You and that horse. Sometimes I think you love her more than me."

Rose chuckled. "That's ridiculous, Mother. I love you just a little bit more." To her surprise, her voice sounded almost normal. Inwardly, there was not one thing that seemed even remotely normal. She avoided looking at her mother because her cheeks felt like they were on fire. "I'm going to change and then I'll be back to help you with dinner," Rose said as she rushed to her room.

"Aunt Maggie would be mighty pleased to see you wearin' that fancy riding outfit, even if there is nobody else around to see how pretty you look

in it," Colleen called out to her daughter just before she disappeared into her bedroom.

By the time the Adair family had settled down for
dinner, Rose was beginning to recover from her
encounter with the Ute brave.

"What kind of trouble did you get into today,
Rosie girl?" Paddy Adair joked as Rose served him
coffee. "Whoa there, that's enough," he said as he
gestured for her stop pouring.

"Sorry." Rose attempted to giggle as the coffee
splashed over the top of her father's cup. "I-I went
for a short ride, just down by the creek." She glanced
at her mother and met her unwavering gaze. Her
mother's hair was a light shade of brown, but her
eyes were the same vibrant blue hue as her own.
Rose looked away quickly.

"You know how I feel about you riding out there
alone. It ain't safe, even if you are on our own land.
Them Ute, they still think they own the entire
country."

"I know, Father," Rose answered quickly. "I am
careful. Believe me, the last thing I want to do is to
encounter any Indians." Her voice trembled slightly,
so she quit talking and turned away without offering anyone else a coffee refill.

The lantern that sat in the middle of the long
wooden table cast a golden haze on Paddy Adair's
pale red hair as he shook his head and added, "I
heard Agent Meeker has them Injuns all stirred up
again and that he's been writin' letters to the army
askin' for help in case of an uprisin'. That could

mean bad news for folks like us. We'd be sittin' ducks out here in the middle of nowhere if them Ute decided to start a war."

Rose set the coffeepot down on the counter but did not turn back around toward the table. Her father's words spun through her mind. The rest of the conversation about the possibility of an Indian revolt was lost to her as she was engulfed by a deep sense of humiliation. Her foolish actions could put her entire family in terrible danger. She could never allow herself to go to the Ute racetrack again, and somehow, she had to find a way to escape from the strange longings she had felt when the handsome warrior had enslaved her in his strong embrace.

Chapter Four

It had been two days. White Owl had been so certain that the girl would come back. The fact that she thought she could ignore him made his blood boil. He had come here today because in two days' time he would begin the *tagu-wuni*, meaning "standing thirsty." For four days until the end the Sun Dance, the most important ceremony of the year for his people, he would not eat or drink anything. He would not be able to leave the Sun Dance lodge until the end of the festivities. He could not wait that long to see his Wild Rose again.

Finding her family's land had not been that difficult once he crossed Milk Creek and headed northeast. He had come upon a block of rock salt that had been put out for cattle—a sure sign that there were white men in the area. Utes did not bother with such unnecessary luxuries for their livestock. When he came across a sizable herd of cattle, he had no doubt that he was getting close to one of the homesteads that were springing up on what used to be Ute land.

A couple of riders had forced White Owl and his pony to hide behind a cluster of large boulders.

As the two men—one older, one younger—had ridden past, White Owl was certain he was on the right property. Both men had red hair and pale complexions, but the younger of the two almost looked like a male version of his Wild Rose. Beneath his wide-brimmed hat, the boy's hair was the same stunning shade of red and curled around his ears and at the back of his neck in the same manner that her curls tumbled down to her waist.

Once the men were out of sight, White Owl headed in the direction they had just come from. He had no doubt that he would come across the house before long. His predictions were correct again. After riding a short distance farther, he topped the crest of a small hill and glimpsed the fields of crops that had been planted for food. His mouth drew into a frown.

Anything to do with farming did not appeal to the Utes, which was one of the reasons they were fighting with the agent at the White River Indian Agency. He was trying to convince the tribe to learn how to plant crops. They preferred to race their ponies rather than spend time hoeing a field. What made the matter even worse was that Nathan Meeker thought the lush meadow where the Ute horse track was located would be a perfect place for planting the crops. White Owl pushed this unbearable thought from his mind and concentrated on the reason he was here.

Beyond the crops was a sprawling house, barn, and corrals. All the larger structures looked new, and a couple smaller outbuildings were in the process of being erected. Wild Rose's family was not poor, White Owl determined. Maybe she really was like the rich, hateful women he had met in Denver.

No, he had not gotten that impression, and White Owl felt that he was usually good at judging people. However, he had been certain that she would come back to the racetrack to see him yesterday, and he had been wrong about that.

Only a few minutes after he had stopped on top of the ridge, White Owl saw someone exit from the house. His heart felt as if it had just risen up to his throat. It was her . . . his Wild Rose. There was no doubt in his mind because his keen eyes could make out almost every detail. Her hair was in a tight bun at the back of her head, but the red hue shined like fire in the morning sky. She moved at a brisk pace, and the full skirt of her blue gingham dress swirled around her legs as she walked. There was something in her hand, but White Owl could not tell what it was.

Although he had no way of knowing whether there was anyone else in the barn with her, White Owl was not in the mood to wait any longer for another opportunity to see Rose. He spotted a good location in a thicket of aspens to hide his pony. He didn't bother to tie the horse up, because Niwaa—meaning "friend" in Ute—was the most loyal mount he had ever possessed. He would trust his life to the sleek black stallion.

Making his way down the embankment, White Owl knew that he was not being wise. He was visible most of the way, and a rifle could be aimed directly at him. Still, he continued his descent until he was at the wide entrance to the barn. He paused at the side of the doorway with his back against the rough-hewn logs. Cautiously, he leaned to the side and glanced into the dim barn. The sunlight that shone through the front entrance was the only light, and the sides and back of the building were too dark to make out anything.

But then White Owl heard her voice. She was talking to someone—or something. He unconsciously put his hand on the wood-handled knife that hung from a belt around his waist, then stepped slowly into the semidarkness of the barn. The strong smell of hay and horse manure assaulted his nose as he slipped into one of the empty stalls at the front of the barn.

"Hello? Is that you, Donavan?"

White Owl crouched down when he heard her call out. She had obviously heard him, too, but she thought he was someone named Donavan. White Owl gritted his teeth together and tightened his hold on the knife handle. Who was this Donavan? Could she have a husband? He had not thought of that possibility before now. The idea prompted a bolt of jealousy. It did not matter if she had a husband already. He would just steal her from him.

"Must be hearing things, Molly girl."

She was talking to her horse, White Owl realized. He released his grip on the knife. She was good to her pony, and he thought that meant that she also had a good heart. As quietly as he could,

White Owl rose and began to move toward her voice. There were three stalls on each side of the barn, and she was in the third stall on the right-hand side. A lantern hanging from a nail inside the stall cast a small light around the interior.

Once White Owl had reached the stall where she was brushing her mare's mane, he did not waste one second. He lunged into the stall, grabbed the girl from behind and immediately clamped his hand over her mouth. She did not even have time to scream. With his other hand, he yanked her up against his body; it was impossible for her to escape.

White Owl could almost feel the fear that radiated from her as her breaths were hitting the inside of his hand in short rapid gasps. Her body was rigid and unmoving, but he knew from their previous encounter that she was capable of putting up a valiant fight, so White Owl did not give her a chance.

Pressing his mouth close to her ear, he said in a low tone of voice, "Do not fight me and do not scream. I will not hurt you."

She did not respond for a moment, then slowly she nodded.

"I will release you, but if you scream or run, you will only be putting your family in danger," he added.

She nodded again, but White Owl did not release his tight hold on her just yet. With his face pressed against her head he was relishing the sweet smell of whatever it was that she used to wash her hair. He was reminded of the intoxicating scent after a summer rainstorm in the deep forest. If only he had time to pull the hairpins out of that prim little bun.

"I will trust you not to scream," White Owl said. "And you will trust me that I am not here to harm you or your family. If anyone is hurt, it will only be because you did something foolish."

She nodded again, this time even more vigorously.

White Owl loosened his fingers from her mouth and exhaled a relieved breath when she didn't start yelling for help immediately. She did nothing—she remained unmoving with her back still to him—even when he pulled his arm from around her waist. Finally, White Owl grasped her by the arm and turned her around so that they were facing each other. Her face was void of any color, and her wide, luminous blue eyes brimmed with tears.

"Listen to me when I say that I do not plan to hurt you or your family," he repeated.

"Wh-what do you want?" she stammered in a voice that was barely more than a hoarse whisper.

"You." He said the single word almost painfully.

Her eyes grew even wider, and if it was possible, her complexion paled more.

"M-me? Why?"

White Owl could barely hear her raspy voice. How could he explain something to her that he did not understand himself?

"You—you are . . . I don't know. I can't stop thinking about . . ." His voice trailed off. He shrugged his shoulders as he struggled for the answer to her simple question. It was the first time in his twenty-four summers that he had been at a complete loss for words.

They were so close that they were almost touching, but not quite. If White Owl leaned forward no more than an inch, their bodies would make contact. He held his body taut and unmoving. He wished he could just reach out and wipe away those tears that were now falling from those lovely blue eyes and rolling down her cheeks.

"I . . . I," White Owl drew in a deep breath. "There is something about you that touches me deep inside." He put his fist up to his chest and sighed heavily. "Since that first day I spotted you watching the pony races, I could not get you out of my head, even before I saw your face. And now—" he paused, still trying to vocalize the strange feelings she had produced within him.

"Now?" she whispered.

White Owl studied the expression on her face. She was looking at him differently. The terror that had engulfed her a moment earlier was not as evident now, and to his surprise, she seemed curious to hear what he had to say.

"Now?" he repeated. "How does a man explain something that he has never known? But from the first moment I looked into your face, I knew."

"You knew." The breath she drew in trembled, making her lips quiver slightly.

White Owl's gaze locked with hers. He could lean down and kiss her now . . .

"Rose," a voice called out from the doorway of the barn. "Ma needs you."

"Oh my!" the girl gasped. "Hide. You need to hide now!"

For a second, White Owl was confused by her sudden mood reversal, and he was unable to move. But when he realized that she was shoving him into the stall with her little fawn-colored mare, he obeyed. He grunted in aggravation, but the girl's look of warning immediately silenced him. She motioned for him to squat down, and to his own amazement, he complied. The instant he had crouched down, however, he grabbed his knife from its fringed sheath and raised it up in an attack position.

"I'm coming, Donavan. Tell Ma I'm on my way."

Donavan! White Owl rose slightly to get a look at his adversary. He instantly ducked back down. Inwardly, he had to laugh at himself. Donavan was definitely not her husband.

"You go tell Ma, I'll finish brushin' Molly," he said.

"No! I mean, I'm already done brushing her. I'll be in the house in a minute."

White Owl could tell Wild Rose was fighting to control her panic, and he thought she was doing a good job. If she could get rid of the boy, he still planned to kiss those lips before he left here today.

"Well, then you can go see what Ma wants."

An exasperated sigh emitted from her. "Okay,

I'm going, but would you go get Molly some fresh water? Here's her bucket."

White Owl saw the girl's arm reach around the door of the stall to grab the water bucket. He helped her out by handing it to her. He heard her gasp, but she quickly recovered.

"Thanks, Donavan. I'll owe you."

"I'll remember that," the boy said as he grabbed the bucket and started back out of the barn.

The instant he was out of sight, she twirled around to face White Owl again. "Please, you have to leave here," she pleaded in a frantic voice.

"Not until you agree to meet me later."

Her head shook negatively in a frantic gesture. "It's too dangerous. But please, don't hurt my fam—"

White Owl refused to listen to her insistent worries that he was going to slaughter her family. He could not think of any way to shut her up, so he let his natural instincts take over.

Any sense of rationality had left Rose. The Ute's appearance in the barn had rattled her to the point of insanity. But when he grabbed her and pulled her roughly against him, she truly had thought that her end was inevitable. Then she realized it was her warrior, and though she still feared his prowess, she also somehow knew that he wasn't there to hurt her. The feel of his lips on hers was the most delicious sensation she had ever experienced.

As his kiss continued to engulf her senses, Rose forgot that they were standing in the middle of the barn and her little brother would be returning at any second. The thought that her father and twin brother, or even her mother, could walk in at any moment never even entered her mind. All her attention was focused on imitating his actions by opening her mouth slightly and letting his lips assault hers with a hunger that made her entire body ravenous for something that she could not begin to comprehend.

Rose allowed herself to revel in the feel of his strong embrace. Nothing outside this moment existed. When he finally began to ease his mouth away from hers, she longed for more.

She stared up at the tall brave, and their gazes locked. Her lips still raged with the fire of his kiss. There were no words that could explain the feelings that gripped her body and soul. From the way he was looking at her, Rose could not help but feel that he was as confused as she was.

The sound of footsteps snapped Rose out of her trance. "You've got to get out, now!" she demanded as she glanced at the doorway. No one was visible yet, but Rose knew that it was probably Donavan returning with Molly's water.

"You will meet me later?" the Ute asked.

"No—I can't," Rose insisted. She looked at the barn entrance—Donavan was walking toward the doorway. In a matter of seconds he would be in the barn and see them. "I'll meet you," she said hastily.

"Where?"

Donavan was nearly to the door. Rose pushed the man back into the shadows of the barn. "I'll meet you at Milk Creek as soon as I can get away." Rose spun around on her heels and ran toward the entrance of the barn. Donavan was walking in just as she reached the doorway. She fought the urge to look back over her shoulder to see if the Ute was still in sight.

"I thought you went to help Ma," Donavan said in an accusing voice.

"I'm going," Rose yelled more harshly than she planned.

She rushed past her brother, but once she was outside the barn, a terrible fear engulfed her. What if Donavan encountered the Ute in the barn and decided to try to fight him? He was her baby brother, and she could not endure the idea of anything happening to him. He had just turned thirteen years old this summer, and unlike her twin, Tate, she and Donavan had always been very close. Leaving him alone and defenseless with the Indian was not something she could do, even though she did have the feeling the Ute had meant it when he said he didn't come here to hurt anyone.

Frantically, Rose twirled around and began to run back into the barn. She practically ran smack into her brother as he was heading back out of the barn.

"You still haven't gone to the house to see what Ma needed?" he said, shaking his head. "Hey, Rosie, are you all right? You look like you're sick or some-thin'.'"

Rose exhaled heavily. Right now, she was feel-ing kind of sick. She glanced toward the back of the barn, but luckily, there was no sign of the Ute. How could she be so desperate to see him again already?

"I'm better now," Rose answered, but she heard the quiver in her voice when she spoke. She just hoped Donavan wouldn't notice.

"You sure? 'Cause you sound kinda funny, too."

She turned away as she tried to calm her racing heart. "Come with me to see what Ma needs," she said. She began running to the house, hoping Do-navan would follow.

"Why?" he hollered.

"Because I said so!"

When Rose reached the front stoop, she turned around and sighed with relief to see that her little brother was ambling toward the house. His pout didn't matter. All that mattered was that he was safe. She just wished she could feel safe again.

She ran her tongue along her swollen lips, which still clung to the taste of the Ute's demanding mouth. The inferno that burned inside her body continued to rage out of control, and her mind was spinning with contradicting thoughts; she could not go meet the Indian at Milk Creek because she could not trust her own emotions around him. Yet for the sake of her family's safety, she had no choice but to go. At least, that was what she kept telling herself.

"Oh, dear Lord above," Rose whispered to herself. "Please give me the strength to make up for my foolishness." She gingerly touched her lips with the tips of her fingers, adding, "Whatever I might have to do."

Chapter Five

She was shaking too hard to saddle Molly, so Rose just put a bridle and reins on the mare before she hoisted herself up and galloped away from the barn. It had been easier to get away than she thought it would be. Her mother had only needed her assistance for a few minutes and had seemed distracted when Rose told her that she was taking a short ride.

Donavan had already forgotten about her strange behavior. She saw him heading into the field behind the barn with his shaggy black dog, Pepper.

As she headed for Milk Creek, she realized she would be utterly at the mercy of the Ute warrior. So why did she feel so . . . so excited?

Milk Creek was only half its normal depth at this time of year, but the water that did flow had a steady current. Heavy thickets of willows, an occasional oak tree, and almost impenetrable bushes lined the sides, but there were many places where sandy beaches edged the gently flowing water. Rose had also discovered hidden little areas in the dense trees where she and Molly could relax in the shade and listen to the lulling sounds of the creek nearby.

Since she had no idea where the Ute would be, she rode to the closest point and figured she would wait until he found her. She had barely halted Molly when she heard him call to her.

"You came—I was not sure you would."

Rose remained on her horse's back and glanced over at the bushes where he had just emerged. She narrowed her eyes as she looked at him. "I didn't have a choice, did I?"

The Indian shrugged. "Yes, but you chose this one."

Rose held her breath as he walked toward her with a swagger that she thought was particularity arrogant. As she watched him approach, she could not help noticing once again what a handsome man he was. His raven hair was parted down the middle, and a folded black scarf was tied around his forehead—the ties hung halfway down his back and almost blended in with his thick waist-length hair. His chest was covered by a loose-fitting V-necked white tunic. A black belt hung low on his hips, and a fringed knife sheath hung along one of his thighs. High suede moccasins with long fringe were tied up to his knees, and his tan cloth leggings were tucked inside.

Rose's gaze moved back to his face when he was only a few steps away from her. She exhaled the breath she had been holding in one big rush. His eyes were the blackest black, and they were surrounded by thick, long lashes in the same midnight hue. Eyebrows equally as dark were perfectly shaped over his eyes, and his nose had a slightly regal hook, which, along with his high cheekbones and full lips, embodied his Indian ancestry. Her heart thudded wildly in her breast.

"Do you like what you look at?" he said with a smug smile.

Rose was snapped out of her daze immediately. He reached out to help her down from her horse. When she hesitated to take his hand, he grabbed her around the waist and stood her on the ground before him. Rose teetered for a moment and avoided looking up into his eyes again. She was so filled with conflicting emotions regarding this man that she could not trust herself to do anything.

"Did I not just prove to you that I didn't come here to hurt you or your family?" he asked in an irritated tone.

"Yes, well, I suppose . . ." she said. The idea that he would try to kiss her again was turning her into a blubbering idiot. His hand cupped her chin and lifted her face up so that she had no choice but to look into his eyes again. Rose's world beyond this moment ceased to exist.

With his hand still gently holding her chin, he said, "I only come to see you. It's time you start to believe me. I do not lie."

I do, Rose thought. *Every time I try to tell myself that I don't want to see you again.* But she did not trust herself to speak. His words seemed so sincere, and she believed him, in spite of every thing her father constantly said about how evil the Ute Indians were.

"Are you going to say something, or do I scare you so much that you have no voice?"

Rose drew in a slow breath. His touch felt so gentle. How could that be? According to her father, his people were ruthless killers. She could not think straight.

Finally she said the only thing that she could think of, "So why do you speak English so good?" she asked once again.

He dropped his hand, releasing his hold on her chin, and to Rose's surprise, he tossed his head back and laughed. It was not a cynical laugh, but one that sounded as if he really did find her question funny.

"I think you are truly worried about that since you have asked me that question several times." He shook his head and smiled down at her. "I will tell you more about me, if you tell me more about you."

Rose still did not move. She continued to stare up at him. His long, thick hair was hanging over his shoulders on both sides of his face, reminding her that he really was supposed to be a savage. Yet his sparkling eyes and jovial smile made her realize that he was just a man . . . a handsome, intriguing, maybe even tenderhearted man, who made her insides smolder with unknown longings and left her lips yearning for another kiss.

He tilted his head slightly. "As a child, I was taken to Denver to live with a Christian family so that I could learn the ways of the white man. I went to their school and attended their church, and learned as much as I could so that I could return to my homeland as fast as possible." His tone grew gruff as he added, "I am a Ute, and no matter how much they tried to make me white, I will never forget who, or what, I am."

His expression had grown hard, and the glint in his eyes no longer looked happy. Rose swallowed over the heavy lump in her throat. She wished she had not pushed the issue. "I am from Denver," she said, trying to change the subject. "Before that we lived in New York for a few years, but I was born in Ireland." She added, "Then we homesteaded here, and I hope I never have to leave. I love it here."

Unconsciously, her gaze roamed out over the landscape and a smile touched her lips. Her nervousness made her babble on. "My father's family still lives in Ireland, though. But my mother's family moved to America with us, and they stayed in Denver when we moved here. My aunt is a schoolteacher, and my grandparents own a general store."

She drew a deep breath and paused. Although she knew the Ute was watching her intently, Rose was unable to decipher his mood.

"Tell me more about you—just you?" he said, obviously not wanting to talk about the people she had just mentioned.

"How many summers—I mean, years—are you?"

"Eighteen," Rose answered, then added, "I have a twin brother. We'll be nineteen in December."

His smile returned. He remembered the two

men he had observed earlier. No wonder the younger one had looked so much like his Wild Rose. "And Donavan, he is your little brother?"

"Yes," Rose said.

"Are there others here?"

"Just my parents," she replied. An uneasy flutter developed in the pit of her stomach. Why was he so interested in her family? As if he sensed her thoughts, his next words helped to calm her growing fear.

"I only ask because I want to know more about you, so you can stop worrying—again."

Rose attempted a weak smile. "Well, you did threaten to kill my father that first day."

White Owl emitted an aggravated grunt. "Will you remind me of that for the rest of our lives?" he asked.

His question made Rose feel weak-kneed and shaky. The rest of their lives? They had barely met, and he was making reference to the rest of their lives?

"I-I don't even know your name," she said in voice that was hoarse.

A smile reclaimed his lips. "I am called White Owl."

"White Owl," Rose repeated. "That is a noble name."

That strange yearning erupted inside her again. They were close enough to kiss . . . again. She cleared her throat and attempted to turn away from his piercing gaze.

"I am a noble man," he said. "And I have named

you Wild Rose." He tenderly took her chin in his hand once again and turned her face back toward him. "Your lips are the color of the sweet pink wildflowers that grow in the meadows."

Rose swallowed hard again, and looked into his dark gaze. "W-well, Rose is my . . . I mean—Rosaline is . . ." Her words faded away as White Owl dipped his head, bringing his lips toward hers.

"My Wild Rose," he whispered as his mouth claimed hers once more.

Although she had waited for this kiss, there was no way Rose could even begin to imagine how deeply his touch would affect her. She became lost in these new emotions. Her lips responded as though they were insatiable. She returned his kiss with no thought of the consequences; that is, until a tiny bit of reality seeped into her spinning thoughts. She pulled back slightly, and with a trembling breath, whispered, "I shouldn't be—we shouldn't be doing this a-again."

White Owl's fingertips gently traipsed along the outline of her kiss-swollen lips. "It is what a man and woman do," he said softly.

"But it's not right for us to be doing this," Rose responded in a raspy voice. The way he was touching her mouth was almost as sensuous as his kiss, and it was making her entire body grow weak with desires that she had never known before.

"If you want it, Wild Rose, it is right," he said as his fingers slid up the side of her face and into her hair, pulling out the two hairpins that held the bun at the back of her head. The long red tresses tumbled down her back in reckless abandon.

Rose gasped. His touch was so gentle. Everything she'd ever heard about Utes told her she should run. Yet it was impossible to pull away. "Even if I did want this," Rose said in a shaky voice, "it is not possible for us to be together, not now, not ever."

"Why? Because I am an Indian?"

Rose heard the cold edge of his voice, and the gentleness of his touch hardened as he gripped the long hair that hung down her back. "Because you, a white woman, are too good to be with an Indian?" he spat gruffly.

"No, no! That has nothing to do with it," Rose gasped. "I do not care that you are an Indian, but my father—"

"Him again," White Owl said through gritted teeth. He started to say more, but instead, he released his tight hold on Rose's hair and stepped away.

His unexpected retreat left Rose more confused than relieved. She watched him mutely when he turned away from her. Presented with his back—and his silence—Rose knew that she should be worried that her words would make his threats to kill her father even more of a reality.

"Please don't hate my father. He doesn't understand that we are all the same, Indians and whites alike."

A cynical chuckle was White Owl's reply as he continued to stare off in the distance. Even as Rose stepped closer to him, he did not turn around to look at her again.

"I will make him understand," Rose added as she put her hand up on his shoulder. Even as she said the words, her mind was in turmoil over how she could ever hope to achieve this impossible task. Paddy Adair was not going to understand any of this . . . Rose didn't even understand any of it herself. She should be scared out of her wits to be here alone with this dangerous man, but all she really wanted to do was feel his gentle touch again.

White Owl turned slowly around to face her again. "I do not know this man—your father, but I have known enough white men to know that he will never understand why we are together."

"Together?" Rose asked. "Are we—together?"

He took one of her hands—it seemed so small and fragile in his own large, rough hand. Her porcelain skin looked even paler against his. "Ever since I first laid eyes on you, I knew that I had to make you my woman. It was a feeling that was stronger than anything I have ever known before, and I am a man who goes after what he wants." He pulled her close to him and let his gaze meet hers, as he added, "And, my Wild Rose, I want you."

Chapter Six

Rose's thoughts were spinning nearly as frantically as her heart was pounding in her breast. This was happening so fast. She still had to come to terms with all that it would mean to her and to her entire family if she and White Owl were truly going to be together. And what did "being together" even mean? She leaned back before he had a chance to kiss her again. "We need to talk more about this. My father, he—"

"That man again!" White Owl interrupted with clenched teeth. His anger glistened in his raven eyes. He pulled his arms from around her waist and dropped them down at his sides.

"Please try to understand why we have to take this slow," Rose pleaded. "You're saying things like 'the rest of our lives' and that you are going to make me your woman, but—"

White Owl turned away from her. "I understand enough," he answered. He started to walk to his horse.

As Rose watched him grab his reins, her uncertainties continued to race through her mind. "Wait," she called out. "Don't go—please?"

White Owl was about to climb on the back of his horse, but now he stopped and turned slowly around to face her again. "Don't tease me, woman," he said flatly.

Rose attempted to ignore his arrogant attitude and reminded herself that she should be counting her lucky stars that he hadn't acted like the savage that he was supposed to be—a thought that made her lips throb with the memory of his kiss and her knees grow weak and shaky again. She drew a deep breath as she tried to calm the racing of her heart. She wished he would leave; she wished he would stay; she wished he would kiss her again. "I want you, too, but—," she shrugged and exhaled sharply.

White Owl's eyes narrowed slightly, but he did not speak for a few seconds. Then he turned and pulled himself onto the back of his horse. He urged his mount forward. As he passed Rose, he said in a nonchalant tone, "You will come to me next time."

His smug smile made her want to scream, but her voice came out hoarse and shaky when she called out after him, "I won't come." She cleared her throat gruffly, and yelled out louder, "I won't come to you."

But he was already halfway across the creek.

"I won't," Rose repeated in barely more than a whisper.

She watched him ride away. His long hair flowed away from his back in the gentle breeze, and his muscled body moved gracefully with his horse as though they were one unit. An odd feeling overcame Rose as she watched him disappear from view, a strange tightness in her stomach that seemed to grow more intense once she realized that he truly was gone.

Unconsciously, Rose rubbed her stomach and exhaled the breath that she hadn't even known she had been holding. She swiped angrily at a teardrop rolling down the side of her face. She had no intention of going to him as he had so boldly predicted. But now, a crushing feeling of sadness washed over her at the idea that she might never see him again.

"Rosaline! What the dickens are you doing way out here?"

Spinning around at the sound of her father's booming voice, Rose almost lost her footing and fell over. At the last instant, she was able to steady herself and stay upright. She glanced at her father and twin brother riding toward her, then back over her shoulder. Thank the Lord above, White Owl was nowhere to be seen.

"I swear, girlie, you are just lookin' for trouble," Paddy Adair yelled as he and Tate rode up to her. He did not give her a chance to say a word before he slid down to the ground to stand in front of her and began to shake his finger in her face. "I've told you again and again how dangerous it is out here with them savages still thinkin' they own this entire country."

"Father, I was just going for a ride." Rose stole a

quick glance up at her brother and noticed the smirk on his lips. She quickly looked back at her father. His pale complexion was flushed dark red.

"You just don't understand, do you?" Paddy said in a voice that barely controlled his fury. "I am trying to save your hide, and if you keep defying me every chance you get, you're gonna end up being kidnapped and . . ." Paddy shook his head vigorously and added, "I don't even want to say the words out loud."

Rose lifted the long skirt of her dress and took a step closer to her father. "I am not in any danger here. The Utes are not violent peop—"

"You really are crazy if you believe that," Paddy interrupted. "They'd rather slit your throat than look at you, and the sooner you realize that, the better off you'll be." Paddy glared down at his daughter.

Rose opened her mouth to disagree, but the expression on his face convinced her to remain silent. She lowered her head down and gave a weak nod. If they had ridden over the ridge just a few seconds sooner they would had seen her talking to the Ute warrior. A shudder shook through her body. This time she had been so lucky, but she could never let it happen again.

"Get yourself home," Paddy said in a softer tone. "Tate will go with you."

Rose tossed her head back up and without looking at her brother stated, "I don't need him to take me back. I promise I will go straight home."

Paddy shook his head. "No, old man Raymond said he saw a Ute buck ridin' down here by the creek earlier today."

"What?" Rose gasped. Paul Raymond was their nearest neighbor, and somehow he must have seen White Owl. "That is not . . . I haven't seen anyone." Rose heard the quivering in her voice as she lied once again to her father.

"Thank the Lord for that. But," Paddy shook his finger at his daughter again, adding, "next time you might not be so lucky." He motioned with his hand in an impatient gesture. "Tate, get your sister home, now."

Rose saw her father's hand move up to where his rifle was holstered on the side of his saddle. He unhooked the safety strap before pulling himself up into the saddle.

"Where are you going?" Rose asked. She feared she might start crying once again.

"I'm going after that Injun to make sure he never trespasses on my land again."

The stricken look on Rose's face was lost to her father since he wasted no more time before kicking his horse in the sides and galloping off in a cloud of dust along the creek bed.

It was apparent to Rose, however, that Tate had not missed her reaction. His narrowed blue gaze was leveled directly at her, and his expression was not the least bit friendly.

"What are you up to, Rosaline?" he asked bluntly.

Rose grabbed Molly's reins, and then swung up onto her back. "I'm headed home. Are you coming?" She did not give him time to reply as she urged her horse forward.

Unfortunately, Tate did not let it end there as he rode up next to her. "I know you. There is something goin' on and you'd better be lettin' me in on your secret or else—"

"Or else what?" Rose halted Molly so that she could stare directly into her brother's face. "You'll tell on me?" Rose shook her head and gave Molly a gentle nudge to go again as she added. "You need to grow up, Tate. We're supposed to be adults now."

"Well, you sure ain't actin' like an adult. How many times does Pa have to tell you not to ride out here alone?"

It was hard to argue with her twin when he was right—this time. She sighed and nodded her head. "I know, Tater. Pa is just worried about me. But there's nothing to worry about. The Utes are not violent Indians."

A snide chortle escaped from Tate. When they were younger he would laugh hysterically whenever she called him Tater.

"Have you been hidin' under a rock? Haven't you heard what Pa has been telling us about the trouble at the White River Agency?"

"As long as we don't get involved in that situation, why would it have anything to do with us?" She glanced back over her shoulder, hoping that she could hide her fear. What would happen if her father caught up to White Owl? "Do you think it is wise for Pa to be out there alone?"

"You're worried about Pa being out here alone, but you think it's all right for you?" Tate shook his head in an aggravated gesture. "That Injun is the one who needs to be worried if Pa catches him on our land."

Rose could not catch her breath for a moment. Her father was a brave man, but she doubted that he would be any match for the powerful Ute warrior. She kicked Molly in the sides to urge her into a gallop. All she could pray for now was that White Owl was far enough away that her father could not catch up to him. Then she had to pray that she was strong enough to stay away from White Owl before she caused any more trouble for her and the rest of her family.

Dinner was a quiet occasion that night. Her father—thankfully—had not seen any sign of the Indian he had been looking for, and he seemed too preoccupied with his upcoming trip to the White River Agency to focus on the fact that Rose had disobeyed him again.

"Tate, I want you to go with me tomorrow. Donavan, you can look after your ma and sister," Paddy said as they ate a dinner of chicken soup and homemade bread.

"Can I go with you?" Rose asked, as she did every time he went to the agency. In the entire time they had lived here, she had only been allowed to go to the agency twice with him.

Paddy shook his head. "It's no place for you to be, not with all the trouble that's brewing over there right now."

Rose lowered her head and remained silent. The last thing she wanted to do was to remind him of the events that had taken place earlier that day. She was still thanking her lucky stars that he had not encountered her with White Owl, or, that he had not caught up to him afterward. But his comment just now about the agency not being a good place for her to be seemed ridiculous. There were other women there, so it was obvious that he just didn't want to spend time with her.

"Maybe it would be all right for Rosaline to go along this time," Colleen Adair said. Her unexpected suggestion caused an uncomfortable silence.

Colleen chuckled and added, "What? You don't think me and Donavan are capable of spending a day alone?" She winked at her youngest son. "We can handle this place by ourselves, can't we?"

Donavan rolled his eyes. "I am thirteen now, remember? Them Utes are already considered a man when they are my age."

"Them savages aren't men, Donavan!" Paddy shouted as he banged his closed fist down on the table.

Rose cringed at her father's sudden outrage and glanced over at her mother. The older woman met her gaze. She could tell by her mother's startled expression that her father's reaction to Donavan's comment was as shocking to her as it was to Rose.

"Pa, I'm sorry. I didn't mean nothin' by—" Donavan began.

"It's okay, boy," Paddy answered in a softer voice. "I didn't mean to take my frustration out on you." He smiled slightly at his youngest son, then glanced around at the rest of the family. "It's just that I'm worried, that's all. I didn't bring you all the way out here just so you all could be butchered by them savages."

"Paddy, surely you don't believe it is going to get that bad?" Colleen said. She rose from her chair and walked over to her husband, where she put her hand tenderly on his shoulder.

Paddy sighed deeply and placed his hand on top of Colleen's. "I don't know, maybe I'm getting all worked up over nothin', but when I thought one of them Injuns was on our property today, I knew I was ready to do whatever it takes to make sure that my family is safe."

Colleen sighed heavily, a trace of a smile on her lips. "You are a good man, Paddy Adair. And whatever happens, I want you to know that we all appreciate everything you do for us." She glanced at the three young people sitting around the table and added, "Don't we?"

In unison, the Adair children all nodded and added their words of gratitude for their father's efforts to provide them with a safe haven here in this wilderness.

For Rose, the reminder that her father was willing to sacrifice everything, even his own life, for his family only added to the tremendous guilt she was already feeling.

As she watched the tender exchange between her mother and father, she realized that her infatuation with the Ute warrior must end, in spite of the searing pain that had just burned a hole through her heart.

Chapter Seven

The White River Agency was located in a lush valley known as Powell Park. The Indian agent, Nathan C. Meeker, had recently moved the entire agency eleven miles downriver to the west, so the new agency was still in the process of being built. The move had only worsened the relations between the agency and the Ute Indians. Powell Park was where the Utes pastured their huge herds of horses, and it was also close to their beloved racetrack.

For Rose, the agency was still the closest thing to a real town that she had seen since leaving Denver. Since she was still surprised that her father had actually agreed to let her accompany him today, she was trying to be on her very best behavior. She wore one of her best dresses with a matching bonnet and her white lace-up boots. She had her mother's grocery list in a small silk satchel that dangled from her wrist. Her favorite gold heart necklace was around her neck. It had been a present from her grandparents who still lived in Ireland, and she cherished the delicate piece of jewelry.

Today, she felt completely in control of her emotions and confident that the dangerous obsession she had for White Owl was under control now; at least, it was when his handsome image was not dominating her thoughts.

When her father had announced that he was taking only Rose with him to the agency, Tate had stomped out of the house and disappeared into the barn. Since Rose had no intention of giving her father a chance to change his mind, she was dressed and ready to go in record time. Along the way, they chatted and spoke of unimportant things, such as the purchases they planned to make at the general store and about the drought that had plagued the area this summer. It had been weeks since it had rained. But it was rare that Rose was able to spend so much time alone with her father, and since he seemed to be in a good mood today, she relished every minute of it.

The agency appeared busier than it had been in the past when Rose had been there. There were a couple more buildings being built, and it was beginning to look like a real settlement. At least half a dozen log structures were scattered along the dirt street. In the center of the small square, the American flag waved proudly in the gentle breeze.

Nestled beside the rolling waters of the White River and surrounded by the lush green vegetation of Powell Park, it was such a picturesque setting that Rose was overcome by the beauty of the area. Once again, she was reminded of how much she loved it here. She only hoped the settlement would not continue to grow until there was nothing but rambling buildings and houses like the city of Denver had become.

"I gotta pick up some nails, so why don't you head on over to the store," Paddy said as he halted the wagon in front of the livery stable. The store was only several hundred yards away, so it wasn't far for Rose to walk.

Paddy helped his daughter down to the ground and added, "Get some licorice for Donavan and some hair ribbons or somethin' pretty for you and your ma."

"What about Tate?" Rose asked as she was smoothing down the front of her flowered dress.

"He wants some bullets. I'm gonna stock up for both of us just in case we get any more trespassers."

A chill raced down Rose's spine. She was reminded once again of how foolish she had been to have flirted with the Ute ... and the danger he represented. But it was going to be fine now, Rose told herself. White Owl had been so confident she would seek him out, but she was equally as positive that she would never go to him. If they never saw each other again, that would be the end of it; that is, if her insides would just quit quivering every time she recalled his passionate kisses.

The thought of never seeing White Owl again began to consume her. Rose's footsteps faltered. She rubbed at her chest where a hard knot had suddenly formed. His ebony gaze flashed before her eyes, and the remembrance of his demanding kisses made her lips throb with a yearning she could not deny. As she reached out to turn the knob on the door that led into the little general store, her hand was sweating so profusely she could not turn the handle. She wiped her palm on the skirt of her dress and drew a deep breath before grasping the knob firmly and pushing the door open.

"Well, howdy do, Miss Adair," a friendly voice rang out. "It's been a spell since we seen you here. It's usually just your pa and brother who comes round here for supplies."

Rose forced a smile and nodded at Frank Weber, the man who ran the store. "Good morning," she answered in a tone that sounded more cheerful than she felt. "It's nice to get away from the homestead once in a while."

Frank reached for the list Rose held and carried on polite chitchat as he gathered the staples that Colleen Adair had written down. It was not until Paddy entered the store, however, that the conversation took on a more solemn tone.

"I hear the Ute situation around here is gettin' worse," Paddy said as he selected his ammunition.

"Yep, it's not lookin' good, not good at all." Frank drew a deep breath and exhaled sharply. "Meeker keeps asking for troops to be sent out here in case them Indians decide to start a war."

Paddy shook his head and sighed heavily. "It's gettin' real serious then. I don't mind sayin' that

I'm nervous 'bout being out there on my land with my family. One of those bucks was trespassing on my property yesterday. It's a good thing for him I didn't catch up with him, or one of us would be dead today!"

Rose felt as though she'd just been punched in the stomach. Luckily, she had her back to the two men, and she remained that way for the duration of their conversation about the deteriorating situation between the whites and the Utes. She knew if she turned around to face them that they would see her agony.

What if White Owl decided to come back to look for her again? The next time he might bring an entire war party with him. The pain in Rose's stomach increased. She could not take that chance, she realized. He had told her that she would go to him the next time, and now she knew that he had been right.

It had been only a week since Rose accompanied her father to the White River Agency. But it seemed like a lifetime since she had made the decision to see White Owl again. During the past few nights, she had hardly closed her eyes to sleep. Every slight noise made her certain that White Owl was there. She had spent every day searching the horizons to see if he was riding toward her, and as much as she hated to admit it, wishing that she would see him riding his big black stallion in her direction again.

The belief that she held the fate of her entire family in her hands was making her sick. She could not eat without feeling as though the food was sitting in her stomach like a rock, and her head hurt continuously as horrible images of what would happen if White Owl came back and had an encounter with her father or even one of her brothers. Even worse was the illness she felt when she thought about not seeing him ever again; the opposing fears and emotions were tearing her apart.

She could not put it off any longer. She had to go to him.

Rose knew she could never convince her mother to let her go riding, especially after her father had forbidden her to ride alone again. Her mother was frightened enough to agree with him, so Rose had no choice but to sneak away without telling anyone that she was leaving.

"Come on, Molly girl," Rose whispered as she led her mare from the barn. The boys were out in the field with Pa, and her mother was happily sewing a new blouse with material her sister, Maggie, had sent to her from Denver. The package had been waiting at the agency along with several other pieces of mail from the Adairs' relatives.

Rose did not follow her usual trail to Milk Creek. She could not take a chance that her father and brothers would see her, so instead she took a heavily wooded route that she hoped would be less visible. Although it took her a bit longer, she reached Milk Creek before noon and was riding up the back side of the ridge above Powell Park in time to see the Utes' afternoon horse races.

Rose brought Molly to a stop in a secluded location among the aspen trees before she reached the top of the plateau. She walked the remainder of the distance to the area where she had first encountered White Owl. In the valley below, the Indians were engaging in their usual games, and it was obvious from their whoops and laughter that they were having a grand time. Rose could not help feeling her usual burst of excitement just to see them as they raced their strong horses around the dirt track.

Without realizing it, she stepped farther out into the open area beyond the bushes and trees as she took in the exuberant Utes' carefree games. Watching them now, Rose found it almost impossible to believe that these men were capable of the destruction that her father and the others in the area were so worried about.

Rose didn't realize that she was being watched, not at first, anyway.

But then she saw him.

White Owl had ridden to the edge of the race-track and was staring directly up at her. She was too far away to see his expression, but Rose had no doubt there was a smirk on his face. She breathed deep and waited for him to ride up the hillside.

He wasted no time in ascending. With every step of his horse's hooves, Rose's heart pounded more frantically in her chest. He was bare-chested again today, and the intense summer heat had created a glistening layer of sweat upon his bronzed skin and dampened his long raven hair.

As he drew nearer, Rose was surprised to see

that he was not gloating as she had expected. Instead, he wore an expression that Rose could not decipher, and his dark eyes were so focused on her face that she found it impossible to look away.

White Owl stopped his horse barely more than a couple of feet in front of her, yet Rose still could not move. She continued to stare up into those mesmerizing pools of ebony without one coherent thought in her head. It seemed as if they stared at each other forever before a shout from below finally broke their trance.

White Owl shouted back at the other Ute in his native language. He sounded annoyed. His attention returned to Rose. "Where is your pony?"

Rose motioned toward the area where she had tied Molly. She glanced back down at the group of Indians, who were all watching them now, but strangely, she was not frightened of them. She looked back at White Owl and nodded in response to his gesture for her to get her horse. He followed her and waited quietly as she pulled herself up into the saddle. He motioned for her to follow, and Rose did so without resistance.

He led her down the backside of the ridge, but when they reached the bottom, he steered her in a direction that she had never gone before. Her mind was telling her how crazy she was to follow him blindly, yet her heart was leading the way and she was powerless to stop it. She rode up beside him, and he looked at her as if surprised that she would be brave enough to ride next to him. But his expression also hinted that he was pleased to have her so close by.

They rode without speaking. Riding across the vast wilderness beside this powerful man made Rose experience feelings she had never felt before. Every step that their horses took increased Rose's desire to break free from the constraints of her life, and run as wild and free as the man who rode next to her.

She became aware that they were following the river and entering a thicket of trees. It was in this lush patch of forest that White Owl finally halted his horse. He dismounted, then reached up to lift Rose down. She held her breath again as their bodies touched while he slid her down to the ground in a slow, sensuous manner. He felt taut and mighty against her body, and she was vitally aware of every inch of him as she moved. Rose wished her feet would never touch the ground.

When, at last, he released his hold and stepped back, Rose realized both of them were breathing heavily. They were unable to look away from each other.

"You came back to me," White Owl finally said.

Rose opened her mouth with the intention of telling him that once again she had no other choice if she wanted to keep her family safe. But the words would not leave her lips. For reasons she could not explain to herself, she had lost the urge to try to defend her actions, and the differing sensations that were flooding through her mind and body right now were overpowering every rational thought she had ever had. At this moment, she just wanted to feel his lips on hers again. How much longer would he torture her like this?

She did not have long to wait.

Chapter Eight

At first White Owl had thought he was imagining the look on her beautiful face. Did she really come here because she wanted to be with him? He drew a sharp breath, but was almost afraid to exhale. If she wanted him as badly as he knew he wanted her, he might not need to breathe ever again.

The past week he had engaged in the ancient rituals of the Sun Dance, but his thoughts had been consumed by Wild Rose. As hard as he tried to focus on the importance of the ceremonies and the dancing and bonding with his fellow tribes- men, his attention kept drifting to how her hair shone in the sunlight, how her body had felt against his. He had emerged from the Sun Dance lodge feeling even more unsettled and confused than be- fore. The ceremony was supposed to give him a sense of spiritual power that would bind him to his family and tribesmen and the world around him. Yet White Owl felt disconnected with everything and everyone, because the only one he wanted to bond with was his Wild Rose.

As they faced each other now, he circled his hands around her small waist. She seemed to be holding her breath, too. Since it was the Ute custom to know many women before choosing a wife—or wives—White Owl had been with his share of young maidens. He knew desire and basic human needs, but none of those other girls had made him feel like he did right now. There was no doubt that he wanted to make her his woman physically. But he wanted more than that, too. He wanted it all . . . her body, mind and soul. He leaned forward to kiss those waiting lips.

Her arms welcomed him without hesitation as she reached up to embrace him around the neck. To his shock and pleasure, she was kissing him back with almost as much intensity as he was kissing her. The heat of this kiss created an inferno in all of White Owl's body that he could not extinguish. He crushed her against him, vitally aware of everything about her—the way her fingers were entangled in his long hair, the way her body molded to his as if they were joined, the way her soft, delicate lips felt hot and demanding against his own mouth. In spite of all those other girls he had kissed in his past, including the kisses he had stolen from Wild Rose, this—he realized—was his first real kiss.

White Owl drew in a ragged breath and leaned back slightly so that he could peer down into her face. Her long brown eyelashes fluttered softly as she opened her eyes to return his gaze. Not even the cool azure waters of the high mountain lakes could compare to the brilliance of her blue eyes.

White Owl felt as if she had just possessed him, and it was a spell he never wanted to break.

They stared at each other for a long moment as White Owl attempted to corral his thoughts and emotions. In a normal situation, if a woman had kissed him like this, there would not have been one instant of hesitation on his part. He would have dragged her into the deep grass and taken what she was obviously offering. But this was not a normal situation, and Wild Rose was not just any woman.

His entire body was shaking with constraint, his father's words echoing through his mind. *I do not worry about you, my son. You have never done crazy things that would disgrace me.*

White Owl vowed to himself that he would not rush into this, because there was nothing about this new turn of events that he wanted to chance. He had tried to move too fast the last time they had been together and had nearly scared her off for good. This time, he had to be sure that she really wanted him in the same way he wanted her and that she would not change her mind after they were together. It would be disastrous to the mounting problems his people were already having with the whites, and the way he was feeling right now, it could possibly destroy him, as well. As hard as it was, he had to be strong, and from the way she was looking at him right now, he needed enough strength for both of them.

He cleared his throat, but the hard lump did not

go away. "We should—we could sit in the shade," he finally managed to whisper. She nodded but did not release her tight hold around his neck. White Owl gently pulled her arms down, but he kept ahold of one of her hands as he led her to the nearest clearing beneath one of the large oaks. She followed him without any resistance. He felt like he was strangling on every labored breath, and it sounded as though she was breathing just as heavily as he was.

Effortlessly, he pulled her down into the lush grass under the low-hanging branches of the old tree. Their hands were still entwined. White Owl was still expecting to see her expression turn to fear and panic, but he was the one who kept being surprised. The only thing he sensed from her at this moment was complete surrender.

"I really didn't think you'd come," White Owl said when he felt slightly in control again. Her hat had fallen off at some point during their impassioned kiss, and now her shiny red hair floated softly around her face. He reached out and pushed a rebellious strand away from her cheek. Her skin felt as flushed as it looked.

"I was so sure that I wouldn't," she said quietly.

A very slight smile touched the corners of his mouth. "But you are here now."

She closed her eyes for a moment as if she couldn't believe it herself. "I tried to convince myself I was coming because I was afraid that if I didn't you would come back and hurt my family, but—" She opened her eyes and looked directly at him as she added, "The real reason I came is because I can't stay away from you."

Her words were so unexpected that White Owl almost had to ask her to repeat them. But the look on her lovely face confirmed what he thought he had heard. "Are you sure?" he asked. His gaze studied every contour of her face looking for any indecision. She had to hear the thudding of his heart; it sounded like a thunderstorm in his chest.

"Yes, I am sure."

At that instant, White Owl knew that he had found the only woman he would ever want. But even as this new knowledge flooded through him, so did the reality of their situation.

"Now what?" he whispered as much to himself as to her.

Rose let out a heavy breath and shook her head slowly. "I was hoping you would know."

White Owl was afraid that at any second she would begin to beg him not to hurt her family. But there was still not a hint of fear or indecision on her face or in those mesmerizing blue eyes. He was the one afraid now, however, so afraid that he was only dreaming.

"I guess you're surprised," Rose said after another long pause. She sighed. "Me, too." She squeezed his hand tighter and a smile curved her mouth.

White Owl was completely mute. Her beauty had entranced him. At last, he forced himself to contribute to the conversation, and he started with the one person they could not ignore, "But your father—"

"I know," she interrupted. "I haven't figured that part out yet." Her reddish-brown brows drew together. "I haven't gotten past the part where I want to be with you."

White Owl smiled and pulled her closer and then turned her around so that she was sitting in his lap. She settled back against him without a moment of hesitation. They were a perfect fit. "That is where we start then," he said as he rested his chin on the top of her head. He knew that if he continued to gaze into those hypnotizing blue eyes, or stare at those soft lips, he would lose what little control he had left. This had to be her choice in every way.

He felt her relax against him even more as he wrapped his arms tighter around her waist and breathed in the heady scent of her hair. It was not the scent of perfumed soap, but natural and intoxicating.

"We already know how my family will feel," Rose began. "So what about your family? How would they feel about you being with a white woman?"

Her question caught White Owl off guard. She cared about his family? Obviously she was thinking about a lot of things that he hadn't even thought to consider yet. "I don't care what they think. I do what I want." He felt her body stiffen slightly. He quickly added, "But it is different with my people. We have been forced to learn how to live with the whites. Your people just want to kill us."

The second the words left his mouth, White Owl knew that he shouldn't have said them. Her body became as rigid as a tree trunk, and her shoulders drew back in a defensive manner. "Wild Rose, my words do not apply to us—to you and me. And my father understands my feelings for you."

Rose turned around to look at him. "You have talked to your father about me?"

"He is my friend as well as my father. And he is much wiser than I am when it comes to women." White Owl chuckled at the shocked expression on her face. Then, when he remembered how her father would feel about the two of them together, he realized that there was nothing humorous about this situation.

"What did you tell him?" Rose asked as she leaned back against him.

"That you wouldn't leave my head alone ever since that very first day that I saw you on the ridge above the racetrack," White Owl answered with honesty. Her body relaxed even more.

He had to fight to control the urges that kept trying to escape from his loins. He couldn't forget how she'd reacted the first time that had happened, and even though they had progressed past that point with their heated kisses, he wasn't sure she was ready to go any further—yet. He tried to reposition himself in case his body defied him.

"Tell me about your people," she said.

"What do you want to know?" White Owl placed his chin on top of her head again. This felt so comfortable. It was like they had known each other forever.

"Well, how long have you lived here?"

He couldn't help the laugh that escaped him. "Forever," he replied. "Ask something else."

"Oh," she said in a thoughtful tone, and then asked, "Well, do you—I mean—your people have courtship rituals, you know, like we do?"

Her question once again shocked White Owl. Her thoughts were obviously way beyond his—he could not get past the idea of making love to her in the summer grasses and she was thinking about courtship. He coughed and cleared his throat awkwardly. "I know many ways of your people, but I am not familiar with the white man's courtship," he responded as he tried to rein in his frantic heartbeat.

She didn't seem to notice his odd reaction as she explained. "We meet a man—a suitor, fall in love, and become betrothed, and then after a proper amount of time has passed, we get married. Is that how the Utes do it?"

White Owl ran his tongue over his dry lips. "No." Her silence told him that she was waiting for more details. He sighed. "We find a woman that we like and hide in the bushes and play songs on a reed or tell her riddles. If she likes it, then she will toss a rock at us. That is an invitation to spend the night in her tepee."

Rose was silent for a minute, and then asked, "You are then considered to be . . . together?"

"No, if we enjoy each other, then we stay together. If not, then we keep repeating that ritual until we find a woman we like."

"Oh," Rose said in a strange tone. "It is considered proper to—you know—um, sleep with more than one woman?"

"We have to find a woman, or women that we want to spend the rest of our lives with. How do we know if we don't try out many different ones?"

She gasped, "Women? You are allowed to have more than one wife?" She twisted away from him and scooted out of his lap so quickly that White Owl didn't have time to react.

As they faced each other again, White Owl reminded himself that white men only married one woman at a time. But he still thought it was rather humorous that she was so shocked by the Ute custom. "If it pleases us," he said. The color that rose up in her cheeks was deep red. It made her blue eyes look even more brilliant.

"But I intend to take only one wife," White Owl added quickly. Her eyes narrowed slightly as if she didn't believe him. "Your turn, Wild Rose. Do you have a suitor?"

Her blush deepened. "Me? Oh, no! I mean, who—" She met his gaze and looked down at the ground. Her hands twisted at the material of her skirt.

The smile on White Owl's lips widened. He was certain that she was thinking the same thoughts he was—she definitely had a suitor now—if she wanted one. Neither of them could deny there was something special between them, and he was certain it was much more powerful than anything either of them had ever experienced.

He reached out and picked up one of her hands

that was fidgeting in the folds of her skirt. "My turn again."

She did not look up at him, nor did she make any effort to pull her hand away. "What do you want to know?" she asked.

"Would you consider having an Indian as a suitor?"

White Owl saw the heavy lump that she swallowed in her throat. She was wearing the shimmering gold heart necklace again today, and it accented the movement in her neck. She looked up at him now. "If I was the only woman he wanted."

Something hit White Owl in the thigh. He blinked and glanced down at the ground beside his leg. It took him a second to realize what it was, and his reaction was delayed because of the shock that rendered him speechless for a moment. He had no idea when she had picked up the small rock—barely more than a pebble—but her meaning was clear.

He studied her smiling face for only an instant more. There was no doubt in her eyes or anywhere else on her beautiful face. He leaned forward to seek those sweet-tasting lips again. She met him halfway.

They both rose to their knees, so they easily fit together as their lips sought to feed their desperate hunger. White Owl's kisses were more demanding than ever before. The direction they were headed had become vividly clear, and he wasn't planning to waste any more precious time. He had known since that very first day, and apparently, she had, too. It had just taken her a bit longer to figure it out.

White Owl's hand moved to the back of her head; his fingers became lost in the tangles of her long curls. He pressed his body tighter against hers as his mouth opened to push his tongue between her lips. For just an instant she seemed to hesitate before her lips separated and allowed his tongue to taste the sweetness of her moist mouth. Almost instantly, her tongue began a taunting dance with his, and if possible, their kisses became even more ardent.

White Owl slowly lowered her to the ground. Beneath them the summer grass was full and soft. They lay on their sides as they continued to kiss. With his free hand, White Owl let his fingers trail over her breast and down along her waist and the curve of her hip. She trembled beneath his touch.

He thought to pull back, to ask her if she was really sure this time, but she did not give his thoughts a chance to become vocal. There was no holding back for either of them now.

Chapter Nine

Rose felt him start to pull away, but she could not imagine any distance between them at this moment. The consequences of her actions tried to invade her thoughts. But her mind was overruled by her wanton body and her yearning heart. She had no doubt now that her obsession with the Ute horse races was merely the prelude to her real destination, which was to be with this man for the rest of her life, and she was eager to begin this new life.

In an effort to control her raging emotions, Rose tried to recall the things her mother had told her about being with a man for the first time. What had she said? It was something like, don't think of the pain, it will hurt less as time goes on. Remembering that did not help, so she tried to concentrate on the incredible sensations racing through her body. Before she even realized what was happening, White Owl had the hem of her full skirt hiked up to her hips and her pantaloons pushed up out of the way, and he was rubbing his hand the entire length of her thigh. The feel of his hand on her bare skin was a wonderfully heady sensation.

Rose imitated White Owl's movements. Since

he was wearing only a suede breechcloth it was easy to touch his bare skin. Beneath her tentative fingertips, his muscled thigh felt hard and smooth. She was distracted by the realization that he was fiddling with the buttons at the back of her dress. How could his hands be in so many places at once?

She clenched her teeth together to keep from crying out when she became aware of his rock-hard manhood moving into position between her legs. All of his movements, the demanding kisses, the heated touches, everything, came to an abrupt halt.

"You have changed your mind." It was a statement, not a question.

"Oh no!" she gasped. "No, please, don't stop." She grabbed his head with one hand and pulled his face to hers, responding with a kiss that she hoped conveyed the intensity of her feelings.

A deep moan escaped from him as he ripped the buttons off the back of her dress with one swift motion. In a tangle of flowered material he pulled the dress and her camisole away from her body and flung them into the grass.

He had rolled her on to her back and she was vitally aware that the only thing that separated his engorged manhood from her virginity was the thin barrier of her pantaloons. In her wildest imaginings she had never even suspected that a woman was capable of having such uncontrollable desires. She throbbed and burned with such intense feelings that she could only arch her body upward and pray for release.

White Owl ignored her immediate demands and focused on letting his fevered mouth assault her breasts. His tongue teased and his lips nipped gently on the taut nipples that had instantly responded to his touch. Rose tilted her head back into the soft grass and drew in a shaky breath. This was torture . . . pure, wondrous, fabulous torture!

His lips moved up to her exposed neck and began to bestow more kisses on the soft skin below her chin and around her ears. Her hardened nipples pressed against his muscled chest as he lowered his full weight upon her. His lips continued to move up past her chin and settled on her lips again, while his hand tugged on the waistband of her pantaloons. Rose helped him out by lifting her hips, and in a joint effort, the flimsy barrier joined the dress and camisole somewhere in the deep grass. With one easy movement, White Owl's breechcloth was tossed away, and there was nothing left to separate their fervent bodies.

Rose braced herself for the pain her mother had warned her about. Thinking of her mother at this instant seemed immoral somehow, so Rose quickly concentrated on the way his lips were seeking hers again. One of his hands had worked its way between her legs, and the tips of his fingers were tenderly rubbing her in way that made her want to scream with delicious pleasure.

Her body arched upward as his mouth covered hers, and before she realized it, he was entering her, stealing away her pained cry with a forceful kiss.

The stabbing pain was brief but intense, and she braced herself for more pain when he began to move slowly within her. To her surprise and delight, the pain faded and in its place were a hundred different magical sensations that continued to build until there was a feeling that she could not even begin to comprehend, and it overpowered everything she had ever known in her existence up to this moment.

"I am sorry about your dress," White Owl said in a tone that did not sound all that regretful. He was trying to figure out how to make it stay together, but only two buttons had been left intact, and there was no way to fasten the dress back together. Her delicate camisole was far beyond repair. Rose figured these were just small problems compared to the one she would have once she returned home. The unbridled passion, though hardly gone, was now invaded by the nagging fear and reality.

She had been gone for hours, and it would probably be dark before she reached home. Nothing she could say would pacify her father's rage. She didn't want White Owl to sense her anxiety, though, so she tried to pretend to be calm.

"Maybe I can find a jacket or something in the barn when I get home and no one will notice," Rose said.

"You're worried about your father," White Owl stated.

Rose turned away from him as she slipped into her pantaloons and pulled them up under her dress.

She felt a heated flame in her face and thought how silly it was to feel shy now. Just as she was trying to concentrate on all the incredible things they had just done and not think about her father, she realized White Owl was suddenly behind her, and then turning her around to face him again. Her gaze was instantly drawn to his face. He seemed to know exactly what she was thinking.

"I cannot bear the thought of you suffering," he said as his fingers traced along the line of her jaw. "Don't go back. Stay with me."

His words, though completely unfeasible, meant more than Rose could even begin to tell him. Oh, what she wouldn't give to stay with him forever. "I have to go home," she said sadly.

She saw the crushing look filter through his handsome face and wished she could be in two places at once. "I will tell my family about us." Doubt clouded his eyes. "I will. Somehow, I will find a way. And then I'll come back, and I'll never leave again."

His fingers continued to gently rub the side of her face. "It is not that easy, my Wild Rose."

The sadness in his voice and his sorrowful expression made a strange sense of foreboding grip Rose. She drew in a shaky breath. "I will be back," she said in a forceful tone. Why was he acting as if this was their last moments together?

"I will ride with you for a while," he said as he pulled his hand away from her face. "We should hurry before your father comes looking for you."

Rose nodded feebly and headed toward Molly. Before she could swing herself onto the mare's back, his strong hands had grabbed her around the waist and lifted her up to the back of her horse. She leaned back down and kissed him without hesitation. Her long hair engulfed them both. Their lips lingered together for a moment after the kiss ended.

They rode side by side in silence until they reached the trail along Milk Creek, where she crossed over into her parents' land. The sun was starting to set in the western sky. Rose felt like something inside her was about to explode. They had just shared the most extraordinary experience a man and a woman could share, and yet they could not find anything to talk about now. Did he already regret what had happened?

"This is as far as I go," he said, breaking in on her worried thoughts.

Rose couldn't stand it one second longer. His lack of communication for the long distance that they had ridden together had fueled her imagination, as she spat, "I guess I didn't pass the test, so now you can just move on to the next willing girl until you find one that you like. That's how it works, isn't it?"

"What are you saying?" He was off his horse now and pulling her down from Molly's back.

Rose attempted to get away, but his grip on her arms was almost painful and she could not move. His sudden movement did not frighten her, but the anger it caused rushed through her like hot lava. "That is how it works, isn't it?" she repeated through gritted teeth.

She glared up at him, waiting to hear his excuses and expecting to see this truth on his face. Instead, his dark features were contorted in pain.

"I have no intention of being with another woman after today," he replied.

Rose peered into his ebony gaze, but she could not read his thoughts. "Then why are you acting so strange?"

He released his hold on her and hung his head down in a defeated manner. "I worry because—" He paused and shook his head as he looked back up. "I care too much. I have already broken the promise I made to myself and to my father."

Confusion spun through Rose's mind. "What promise?"

He shrugged his broad shoulders. "That I would not do something that would make things worse between my people and the whites."

Rose stepped back, but Molly prevented her from going any farther. "Then you do regret what happened today," she said in a raspy voice. Her heart felt as if it was shattering into thousands of pieces.

A crooked smile touched his lips. "Wild Rose, I have never regretted anything less in my life than making love to you today. But I can't help worrying that falling in love with you will be the worst thing that could happen to you—and to our families."

"What?" Rose whispered. Her heart skipped a beat. "Did you just say l-love?"

He chuckled. "Love," he repeated. "I know enough to be certain what that word means in your language."

Rose smiled as their gazes locked. "Yes, and it also means that we will find a way to be together— no matter what it takes."

"I love you, Wild Rose," White Owl said hoarsely before he stole away her breath with another intoxicating kiss.

Chapter Ten

The sun had already set by the time Rose rode over the ridge that led to her parents' homestead. She had rehearsed her excuse over and over again, but even to her own ears, it was a feeble and unbelievable explanation. The idea of such a blatant lie made her feel sick to her stomach.

Now, as she watched her father and two brothers riding toward her, she braced herself for the onslaught of anger and accusations that she knew would come.

"Rosaline!" her father yelled as they approached. "We were just getting ready to head over to the agency to ask for help to look for you."

"Where have you been?" Tate spat out. His narrowed gaze moved over her as he shook his head with disgust.

Donavan, dear Donavan, just looked relieved.

"I'm sorry," Rose gasped, focusing her attention on her father. "I-I had a little accident, but I'm fine."

They were all surrounding her now, and she hoped that the daylight had faded enough so they couldn't see the heat raging through her cheeks. Her father's angry expression softened slightly.

"Are you hurt?" he asked gruffly. His gaze raked over her and as he realized that her dress was torn, the look of rage returned. "What happened to you, girl?"

Rose cringed. She had no doubt what he was probably thinking. Now she would discover just how good of a liar she really was. "I took a tumble from Molly, that's all." She tried to sound nonchalant. "I was exploring and—"

"You what?" Her father's voice echoed through the air. "What is wrong with you, girl?" He shook his fist at Rose as Tate decided to give her his opinion, too.

"You are so stupid," her twin hollered. "I think you are hopin' them Injuns kidnap you."

Although she had known what to expect, Rose had no energy left to fight with Tate. She looked back at her father and added, "I'm sorry that I worried you, Pa." She thought about adding that it wouldn't happen again, but that would just be another lie.

Her father was so filled with rage that he was unable to speak. He shook his head and muttered under his breath as he swung his horse around and rode back down the slope. Tate glared at her once more before he followed their father.

Rose exhaled a heavy breath and looked at Donavan. His sorrowful expression caused a sharp pain to rip through her chest as he looked at her.

"I'm really glad you're all right, Rosie," he said quietly. "Ma's been real scared, too."

Tears flooded her vision and burned trails down her cheeks.

Donavan gasped, "What is it, Rosie? Are you really hurt?"

She attempted to stop the guilty sobs as she shook her head vigorously. "I'm fine, Donavan. I just so feel bad that I made everyone worry." The terrible guilt, combined with the overwhelming regret that she might not be able to see White Owl again, was almost more than she could handle and it was impossible to stop the tears.

Donavan moved his horse closer to Molly and reached out to pat her on the shoulder. "It's okay, Rosie. Just don't go ridin' no more."

The agonized sob that shook her body caused Donavan's sympathetic gestures to increase and his gentle pats became more like slaps against her shoulder. Rose knew she had to get her emotions under control, and then she could figure out what she would do next.

"I'm fine, really," she gasped as she took a deep breath. She gently pushed her little brother's hand away from her shoulder. "I need to see Ma and tell her I'm sorry for making her worry." She kicked Molly in the sides as she added, "Thanks, Donavan."

He shrugged and nudged his horse down the incline. By the time they reached the bottom it was nearly dark, but Rose could see her mother waiting on the front stoop of the house holding a lantern. Rose's insides twisted into a tight ball. This was hopeless. She was going to hurt them all so badly. But after today, there was no way she could avoid it.

Donavan took Molly to the barn so Rose could go to her mother's waiting arms. The tears that had started earlier had not stopped, and they only increased when her mother wrapped her arms tightly around her. "I'm so sorry, Mama," she whispered into her mother's ear.

"You're here now, so nothin' else matters," Ma whispered back through her own choked voice.

They lingered on the porch for a moment longer before her mother pulled back and said, "Clean yourself up while I get you something to eat. Then, you can tell me what happened."

Rose shook her head. "I'm not hungry—just tired. And there's nothing to tell really. I rode too far, and then I fell off Molly and"—she motioned over her shoulder—"my dress got ripped. That's all there is to it." She glanced away from her mother as they entered the lighted interior of the house. The lie was not getting any easier to repeat.

"I'll check your back for cuts and bruises," Ma said as she reached out toward her daughter.

"No!" The word was harsher than Rose meant for it to be. "I landed in the grass. I'm not h-hurt." That was almost too close to the truth. Rose turned away from her mother for fear that she would notice. "I'll be in my room."

To her surprise, her mother made no attempt to stop her. This made her feel even worse. Her poor mother had been frantic with worry, and all she wanted to do was take care of her, but Rose had yelled at her instead. She threw herself on the bed facedown and tried to sort through her whirling thoughts. She loved her family, she did, but she couldn't be here any longer. Not now—not after White Owl, because she loved him even more.

She rolled over and stared at nothing as the tears continued to fall. Now her thoughts and worries about her family were invaded by the memory of this afternoon. She shivered and wrapped her arms around herself, but it was his arms that she was remembering . . . White Owl's powerful arms, his smooth, bronzed skin, the way his thick raven hair hung over his bare shoulders, his tenderness as he had taken her on the sensuous journey that transformed her from an innocent girl to a woman—his woman. Her mind became filled with so many sweet, passionate memories of their glorious afternoon. A slow ache worked through her entire body, and an incendiary flame settled in her loins. Nothing could keep her from going back to him.

Breakfast the next morning was strange and awkward. Everyone was polite, but nothing was said about the events of the day before. Rose kept waiting for the fight with her father and Tate to begin: the accusations about her selfishness from Tate and the reminder that she was disobedient and careless from her father. But they said nothing, and Rose grew nervous.

Even her mother was unusually quiet as they

cooked the morning meal of flapjacks and fresh eggs that Rose had gathered earlier from the hen-house. Her mother had asked if she was feeling better when she had first emerged from her room this morning, but that was it—no more questions from anyone else.

Donavan smiled tentatively at Rose as they all settled around the table, but before she could respond, he quickly looked away as if he had been instructed not to speak to her. Rose's uneasiness increased.

"Me and the boys are headed over to the Richards' place to check on that horse they have for sale," her father said as he pushed his empty plate toward the center of the table. He glanced at his wife. "I trust you womenfolk will be safe if you stay close to the house." He did not look in Rose's direction, adding, "The shotgun is loaded."

Rose glanced at the gun by the door as a sense of dread clutched at her breast. She opened her mouth to attempt to make amends about yesterday, but once again, she could not bring herself to make promises that she knew she would not keep. As her brothers and father departed, Rose was left alone with her mother and a chance to apologize. "Mama, about last night, I—"

"Rosaline," Ma interrupted. "I've known you for more than eighteen years. I know there's something goin' on with you, and I know you'll tell me when you're ready." She raised her hand up and shook her head when Rose tried to speak. "All I ask is that you don't do something crazy to get yourself hurt—or worse. I would never forgive myself, or your pa for that matter, if something happened to one of my children because of our decision to come out here to this wilderness. Sometimes I think we should have stayed in Denver."

Rose hung her head and stared at the floorboards as her mother's words spun through her mind. Finally, when she felt she could speak without choking up, she said, "I am sorry, Mother. I don't intentionally want to hurt you or Pa." She glanced up and looked into the blue eyes that mirrored her own, adding, "But we moved here because we wanted to be a part of this beautiful wild country. I want to explore every inch of it and learn everything there is to know." She sighed. "I don't know how to explain to you just how much I love it here. I thank the good Lord above every day that we didn't stay in Denver."

They stared at one another for a moment until Colleen sighed, too. "I was really hoping you wouldn't say something like that, because it would make this all so much easier."

Rose's brows drew together. "What are you talking about?"

"Your pa and I were thinkin' that maybe you might want to go back to Denver and stay with your Aunt Maggie for a spell and—"

"No!" Rose gasped. "Never. I wouldn't go back to Denver."

The look of surprise on her mother's face went unnoticed by Rose as the idea of leaving White Owl brought her to the brink of hysteria. "Never!" she cried out again.

"It was just a thought," her mother said. "I—we didn't know, I mean, we just don't understand why you insist on putting yourself in such danger." She reached out in an attempt to soothe her daughter, but Rose backed away. "I'll try to make your father understand," she added in a worried tone.

Rose took a deep breath, trying to calm her frantic heartbeat. There was no way her family could send her away. If they even suggested it again, she would leave on her own. But she would not be going to her Aunt Maggie's in Denver.

"I won't go," Rose murmured as she backed toward the front door. She twirled around and ran out of the house, not trusting herself to stay with her mother for another minute. She was too close to telling her mother exactly why she refused to leave here, and she knew that she could not blurt out her confession in the heat of anger. She would tell them when the time was right, but she hadn't figured out when that would be yet.

The warmth of the morning sun heated her skin. Tears stung the corners of her eyes, but she blinked and angrily wiped them away before they had a chance to fall. The idea that she could leave here—leave him—was inconceivable. Her stomach twisted with the realization that she could not wait much longer to tell her family that she was in love with a Ute warrior. The opposing feelings of joy and terror made her knees so weak that she had to lean against the front porch rail for support.

Since there was only one place that she could go to think when she was this upset, Rose headed for the barn. Being with Molly was always soothing. The interior of the barn was cool and dim. The smell of the hay and manure filled Rose with a sense of comfort and slightly eased her panic.

She needed to see White Owl and tell him what her parents were suggesting. But unless she really did want to destroy all chances of ever keeping peace with her family, she could not leave here again today.

Once Rose reached the stall where her little mare was munching on several strands of straw, she gave in to the despair that filled her heart. She sat on the stool in the corner of Molly's stall and placed her head in her hands and let the agonizing sobs overtake her body. Less than twenty-four hours ago, she had been happier than she had ever imagined being; she had fallen in love and become a woman in every sense. But now she felt as though her entire world was caving in around her.

"White Owl," she whispered through her tears. "I need you." Molly whined softly, as if trying to comfort her, and Rose instinctively reached up to rub the mare's nose. Molly snorted and whined again as Rose stood up and began to scratch behind her ears. "We have to go to him, Molly," she whispered in the horse's ear. "But we'll wait until tonight after everyone is asleep."

Chapter Eleven

White Owl could not help himself. It was the most foolish thing he had ever done—up to this point in his life, anyway. At least the stupid dog had stopped barking and growling after only a couple minutes. It hadn't even barked long enough to alert the occupants in the house. Now the dog was glued to White Owl's side as if they were old friends. Its tail wagged every time White Owl even glanced in his direction. He snickered and shook his head; he hoped the Adairs were not counting on this animal to alert them to intruders, or they would be in dire trouble.

He forced himself to pat the head of the shaggy dog. "Good boy," he said in an effort to remain in good standing so that the dog would not bark again once he left the shelter of the barn.

The problem of the dog seemed to be resolved, so now White Owl just had to figure out how to get to his woman.

Cautiously, he sneaked out of the empty horse stall where he had taken refuge until he was certain no one was going to come out of the house when the dog had first barked. The only light in the barn came from the faint silver shine of the moon through the partially open door.

His plan was to sneak from window to window until he found her. He was desperate to know what had happened after she had returned home last night. There was little doubt in his mind that she would not be able to come to the racetrack for a while since she had gotten home so late. So he would have to go to her until they could be together all the time.

But before he had even left the barn, the dog was distracted from his petting and turned to look toward the doorway. White Owl wasted no time ducking back into the empty stall. He crouched and waited to see what had drawn the dog's attention. From his hiding spot, he could not see the barn door, but he could hear footsteps approaching. He braced himself against the wall behind the half door of the stall and waited. His right hand rested on the handle of the knife he wore on his hip. When he glimpsed the source of the noise, he slowly exhaled the breath he had been holding and rose from his hiding spot.

Rose's eyes widened at first and she threw her hand over her mouth as she gasped loudly. But almost immediately, she relaxed. "Oh, thank the Lord above, it's you," she said. A smile curved her lips as she stepped closer to him. "I was just planning to come to you," she whispered. She looked up at him with expectation and relief.

For an instant White Owl could only stare down at her. She constantly filled him with amazement.

Even in the near darkness he could see the expression on her lovely young face; she truly seemed happy to see him here. He sighed as his worries about coming to her disappeared. He'd been worried that she might regret what had happened between them the day before. Or what if she had told her father and sent a hunting party after him? But now all of those fears were completely gone.

"I was worried about you," he said quietly. He yearned to touch her soft cheek; instead, he held his hands firmly at his sides. "What happened with your father last night when you got home?"

Rose's smile faded. "That's what I was coming to see you about."

White Owl's hands drew into fists. "What has happened?"

She began to shake her head as she closed her eyes for a moment. "They want to send me to live with my aunt in Denver, but I won't go . . . not now, not ever!"

The meaning of her words hit White Owl hard. He could not imagine not seeing her again. "Because of me they are going to send you away?"

"They don't even know about you, not yet, anyway." She reached out and grabbed his hand. His fist immediately uncurled and their fingers intertwined. "They say it's for my safety because I insist on going for rides in spite of the danger." She squeezed his hand tighter. "If they only knew how much danger I was really in," she hinted suggestively.

White Owl shook his head and smiled again,

but he was still worried. "What if they make you go? I hated my time in the white man's settlement called Denver, but I would go back there to be with you."

Wild Rose's expression grew serious. "No, I will not leave here. I love this land, and I love you. Neither of us could be happy anyplace else."

As he shook his head again, White Owl began to realize that he was fighting a losing battle. The determined look on her face made her position clear.

"You must quit riding over to the racetrack then, at least until we can figure out how to tell them. The time is bad because of the relations at the agency. I will talk to our chiefs and try to find out what is happening between our people and the whites. Until then, I will come here to see you."

He took hold of her other hand and pulled both hands up to his lips and kissed them each gently. She smiled again and sighed softly.

"Will you come every night?" she asked.

His kisses moved to the inside of her wrist. "As long as you want me to come," he whispered.

"For the rest of my life," she replied as she stretched her arm out so that he could kiss all the way up to where the sleeve of her calico dress stopped above her elbow.

"Woman," he sighed. "You know this—us— might not end well." He placed her limp arm on his shoulder, and she wrapped her hand around the back of his head. Her fingers dug into his thick hair.

"No, don't say things like that," she said in a

defensive tone. "You are the best thing that has ever happened to me. I refuse to believe we can't have a happy life together just because we have different colors of skin."

White Owl knew that he wouldn't be able to resist her for much longer. There were so many reasons that he shouldn't be here—and she had just pointed out the most obvious—but there was something so much stronger ruling his actions now. He scooped her into his arms and carried her to the ladder that led up to the loft. It was only a few feet, but she molded herself against him and began to kiss the side of his neck with soft kisses. His knees were shaking by the time they reached the ladder.

He stood her on the second rung, and she turned back around and wrapped her arms tightly around his neck. She was slightly taller than him while she was standing on the ladder, so she took the initiative and let her lips cover his mouth with a hungry kiss that took his breath away as her fingers raked through his hair again. He pulled her against him, nearly taking her off the ladder before they finally parted. It took him a moment to breathe, and he could tell she was having an equally hard time regaining enough composure to turn away from him and climb the rest of the way up to the loft. He followed closely behind, thinking only briefly of the dire consequences if they were discovered here together.

The loft was completely dark as they scooted to the back corner. White Owl was surprised to discover that a mattress awaited them. "Did you put this here for one of your other suitors?" he asked with a chuckle.

Rose huffed indignantly and didn't respond to his insinuation. "This is my little brother's hide-out. But starting tonight it will be our hideout."

White Owl reached out in the blackness until he had her in his arms again. He had never known a woman so willing, and her optimism and passion made his heart feel as though it was going to burst out of his chest. Obviously, her introduction to lovemaking had been more than satisfactory, because she was more than eager to repeat the act now.

Wild Rose slid into his arms without further invitation. Their kisses were more urgent now as they fumbled to remove their clothes. Unlike yesterday, there was not a moment of trepidation.

Wild Rose leaned back as White Owl carefully pressed her down into the mattress. He heard her take a trembling breath as he worked his hips in between her parted thighs. As he entered her, he felt her body tense as if she expected to feel pain again, but instantly, she began to relax. Her hips arched up to meet his movements, and her fingers dug into the skin on his back as their passion grew in intensity. At last they clung together, breathless, satisfied, yet wanting—needing—more.

The threat of morning sun arriving soon signaled the end of the most erotic experience White Owl had ever known. They had been like ravenous animals whose hunger had been unquenchable. He felt like a man possessed as he had made love to his Wild Rose over and over again. To his amazement, her enthusiasm had equaled or even exceeded his at times, and he had never known a passion that even began to compare to this night.

"You promise?" Rose asked.

He chuckled. "I promise," White Owl answered as he lifted her down from the ladder.

The early rays of the sun would be peeking over the eastern horizon at any moment. They had lingered far too long in each other's arms because they had not wanted this night to ever fade into day.

"You must hurry back now," he added, sounding regretful.

A pained expression contorted Rose's face. "I don't think I can hurry anywhere today." She glanced at White Owl as a fire began to burn in her cheeks. Her entire body felt worn out, and she was sore in places that she didn't know could be sore. The fact that they had not slept one minute all night long was beginning to take its toll on her weary mind, too. She yawned and frowned when he laughed.

"Are you sure you want me to come back tonight?" he teased. "Maybe I should let you rest for a day or two."

Rose tossed her tangled hair back over her shoulder. Her lower lip protruded like a spoiled child's. "You promised."

White Owl shook his head in defeat. "You are a demanding woman. But I can't deny you anything." He kissed her forehead and then twirled her around toward the barn door and gave her a gentle shove. "Now, hurry before your father wakes up."

Rose sighed and glanced back over her shoulder, "You will be here tonight." It was a command.

"Do you want your father to shoot me?" White Owl motioned with a wave of his hand toward the door. She gave a resigned nod and started slowly toward the exit. As she reached the threshold, she looked back again.

"I promise," White Owl repeated.

Leaving proved to be more difficult than Rose had imagined. What if something prevented him from coming back tonight? After the night they had just spent together, she was not sure she could survive another night unless she was in his arms.

A loud bark caused Rose to stumble to a halt. She twirled around at the sound of the family dog's sudden outburst.

"Pepper!" she called out through gritted teeth. "Be quiet!"

The black dog stood outside the barn door and stared inside. Rose shook her head in aggravation. Donavan's dog barked at anything that moved and was pretty worthless as a watchdog, because sometimes he didn't bark at all when he should. Earlier this year, they had coyotes sneak into the henhouse and kill half the flock and eat all the eggs. Pepper slept through the entire incident. Now, he glanced back at her, and then turned back toward the interior of the barn and growled.

"Pepper, come!" Rose commanded.

The dog turned toward her again and acted uncertain for a moment before his tail began to wave back and forth. He ran toward Rose as if he had forgotten all about whatever it was that held his attention in the barn just an instant earlier.

She kneeled down and grabbed the dog by the long black fur around his neck so that he couldn't get away as she stared at the barn. She was certain White Owl had already left through the back door, and now the building contained only the unbelievably passionate memories of the night they had shared in the loft.

As she slowly made her way back into the quiet house, she could not wipe the smile off her face. Luckily, there was no one awake yet, and she continued to smile all the way in to her bedroom. It would be a long day, and she hoped tonight would be even longer.

Chapter Twelve

"I am worried, my son."

"You do not need to be," White Owl said. He looked away from his father as he led his horse from the corral.

Beside Strong Elk stood White Owl's brother, Two Feathers. A lopsided grin curled his mouth. "My brother has become an enemy lover," he said.

White Owl twirled around. He was a couple inches taller than Two Feathers, but the younger man stood up as straight as possible so that they were almost eye-to-eye. "She is not my enemy!" White Owl spat. He took a step toward his brother. "But you—"

Strong Elk stepped in between his sons. "Stop!" His gaze moved first to White Owl, then to Two Feathers. "My sons will not fight because of a woman, no matter who it is."

For a moment the three men remained unmoving, until White Owl broke the uneasy confrontation. "You are right, my father. There will be no fighting. This woman is going to be with me forever." He glanced at his brother, adding, "So everyone else will have to accept it."

Two Feathers narrowed his eyes and refused to back down until Strong Elk turned to confront him. "White Owl has a right to love whomever he wants, and you, as his brother, must not question this."

With an angry grunt, Two Feathers took a step backward. "But you just said you were worried?"

Strong Elk relaxed his terse stance slightly. "Yes, I am worried for my son's safety, not who he chooses to love."

"We will all pay the price if someone at the agency hears about them," Two Feathers retorted. His flashing dark eyes focused on his older brother once again.

"No one will find out until we are ready for them to know," White Owl answered, more to his father than to his brother.

Strong Elk shook his head and sighed. "You have been going to this woman every night. Surely her family must notice that she is gone, too? Or are you foolish enough to enter her home while the others are sleeping there?"

"No, where we meet it is safe, and she does not come to me until everyone is asleep." White Owl was beginning to feel like a child who was getting scolded for something he knew he shouldn't be doing.

A worried frown tugged at Strong Elk's mouth. "There will come a time when someone will know. What if she carries your child? How will the two of you hide that?"

White Owl had thought of this possibility a

couple of times in the past few weeks, but he had been too overcome with desire to let it deter him.

"White women are not like Ute women," Strong Elk continued. "Our women do not produce easily, but whites are fertile and already this woman could carry your seed in her."

White Owl had to exhale the breath that was lodged in his throat. He knew that what his father said was true. Ute women rarely had more than one or two children, and many of them never bore children at all. Most white women, however, seemed to have been blessed with the ability to bear hordes of children during their lifetimes. His father could be right . . . it might have happened already. For the past few weeks, they had spent nearly every night exploring and learning more sensuous ways to pleasure each other than he had ever imagined possible. And he was also discovering how much he loved her in every other way.

She was obviously passionate and anxious to learn every way to please him, but they had also spent much time talking and finding out each other's deepest thoughts.

White Owl was amazed many times over by how she loved this great land as much as his own people did, and she honestly felt that the white men were wrong to try to take it away from the Utes. Her compassion for the plight of his people endeared her to him even more. Every time they were together, he found something else about her that made his love for her expand. A child born of their love would bring him more happiness than he could even begin to envision. But it would also mean making their love known to everyone.

With a hard swallow, White Owl turned away from his father and brother and pulled himself up to Niwaa's bare back. "We will face whatever comes." His voice was firm, but inside he was tormented by thoughts of what the future might bring for him and his Wild Rose.

Two Feathers did not bother to respond. He threw his hands in the air and stalked away.

Strong Elk looked up and met his son's worried gaze. "This woman, this . . . ?"

"Wild Rose," White Owl answered.

"Wild Rose," Strong Elk repeated. "She must be special."

As he slowly nodded, White Owl looked off in the distance. "She is, Father. She is."

He nudged Niwaa forward without waiting for a response. He needed to be with Wild Rose as soon as possible, and the sun was already growing low in the western sky. It would be dark by the time he crossed Milk Creek.

The ride seemed longer tonight than it had in the past, perhaps because the conversation he had just had with his father and brother only intensified the feelings he already had for Wild Rose, and he knew that these passionate encounters could not last forever. Soon they would have to think about the future.

As the sun dropped below the horizon, the heat of the late August day finally began to fade. If they didn't get some rain soon, the entire land was going to burn up. He had heard that there were wildfires burning in numerous places around Colorado, and in some instances, the whites were trying to blame the Utes for starting the fires. White Owl grunted with disgust. His people would never destroy the land they loved so dearly. But he could not remember a drought that had lasted so long in this part of the country.

As a child he had lived for a time with his mother's family, the Jicarilla Apaches, in New Mexico. The unusually hot weather this summer reminded him of the heat in the desert of New Mexico. But at least here they had the welcoming shade of the tall oaks and cottonwoods, as well as clusters of aspens that covered the countryside with abundance.

By the time he had reached the secluded area in a thick grove of cottonwoods where he would leave Niwaa, the nighttime temperature had grown cooler. He approached the Adair ranch slowly as his gaze carefully observed every detail that he could make out in the darkness. As had become the habit, Pepper ran out to meet him, tail wagging. White Owl took the time to give the animal a couple of pats on the head.

Everything seemed to be the same as it had been for the past few nights, and knowing that he would soon be holding Wild Rose in his arms made a tremor of excitement race through his body. When he slipped into the dark barn, he was prepared to climb up into the loft to wait for her. She usually showed up a short time after he arrived.

He had barely entered the dark quiet barn, however, when he was almost knocked to the ground. Wild Rose threw herself against him. Her arms wrapped tightly around his neck in a strangling hold. White Owl had barely recovered from his shock when he realized that her attack was not an excited reaction to his arrival. The sound of her sobs made his insides twist. He wrapped his arms tightly around her waist and pulled her closer.

"What has happened?" he asked. He was afraid to think that her father had found out about them, because if this was the case he could probably expect to be shot dead at any moment. He glanced around the dark barn nervously.

"You have to take me with you tonight," she finally choked out through her sobs.

White Owl pushed her away slightly. "Why? You must tell me what has happened? Your father knows—"

Wild Rose shook her head. "No, but it doesn't matter." She wiped at the tears streaming down her cheeks. "H-he's taking me back to Denver, and I won't go!" She stepped back far enough to point at the brown leather satchel that sat by the doorway. "I've packed my things, and I'm going with you tonight. I left my parents a note telling them I had fallen in love with a Ute warrior and that I was going far away from here with him and not to bother looking for me, because they would never find me."

Her words did not sink in to White Owl's thoughts for a moment. But as they did, he realized there was no way he could agree to her plan. If her family found out where she really was, they—and every other white man—would think he had abducted her. "No, that is not possible," he said in a panicked voice.

Even in the shallow light he could see the expression on her face. She turned loose of him and backed away.

"Wait," he said quickly. "I—"

"You don't want me to go with you?"

The disappointment and hurt in her voice was obvious. White Owl felt a pang of guilt in his chest. "Yes, I always want you with me. Do you have any idea how it pains me to leave you every morning?"

She drew a trembling breath. "Then why—"

"Your father and dozens of other whites will come after you," he interrupted. "He will not believe that you came with me willingly, and he will tell the others I took you captive."

"You want me to go to Denver, then?" Another sob shook her body.

White Owl closed his eyes for a moment as the desperation of this unexpected situation twisted through his heart and filled his mind with confusion. He could not even begin to imagine not having her near. The conversation he had with his father kept echoing through his mind.

He opened his eyes and reached out to pull her up to him again. She came without hesitation and placed her cheek against his chest as her arms encircled his waist. "We will have to figure something out." He buried his face in the sweet aroma of her red tresses. No, he could not let her go to Denver, or anywhere else, not without him at her side.

"I can't leave you," she whispered.

"You have stopped riding out alone. Why does he still want to send you away?"

She squeezed him harder. "He thinks there's going to be more trouble between the settlers and the Utes soon. He said he doesn't want to have to worry about me deciding to take off on one of my rides. I promised I won't, but he said his mind was made up. He wants to leave tomorrow morning."

The spot on his cotton tunic where she rested her cheek had grown wet from her tears. White Owl began to caress her long hair in comforting strokes. "Tomorrow?" he repeated. His voice was hoarse, and his heart felt as if it had just ceased to beat.

His thoughts were racing with indecision. He knew the consequences would most likely be dire if he took her to his village tonight. But if he didn't take her with him now, there was no telling when he'd see her again—if ever. This was not an option.

"We should go now," he said in a voice that sounded much more certain than he felt inside. "Get your pony and meet me on the top of the ridge." He turned her loose and started toward the door, but then stopped and turned back around. In two strides, he grabbed her by the arms and pulled her up roughly against him. He brought his mouth down on hers with a sense of urgency that he couldn't explain even to himself. She seemed to sense his mood and threw her arms around his neck again, enslaving him in such a tight embrace that he could barely breathe. Their lips pressed together, hard and demanding.

White Owl wished that they could just climb up to the loft and lose their cares in the pleasure of lovemaking. But tonight change was in the air, and he could only hope that it would not be the beginning of the end for their forbidden love.

Chapter Thirteen

"I'm worried," Rose said as they rode to his village. "I don't want to cause trouble for your family. Maybe we should go up into the mountains for a while."

White Owl gave a sarcastic chortle. "My family—my people—have much worse trouble than us, Wild Rose."

Rose heard him sigh. She felt a deep ache in her heart. She had no idea what to expect when they reached the village, and she didn't want White Owl to know how terrified she was of facing his family and friends. He had talked some about his childhood and the customs of his people, but he had told her very little about his family. Her fear of meeting them was not because they were Indians, but rather because she was afraid that they would not approve of her—a white woman.

They spoke very little as they rode, which only increased Rose's worries. She needed White Owl to reaffirm that they had made the right decision to come with him, but he was solemn and silent. She wanted nothing more than to be with him, but to be with his family and the rest of the Utes in his village was another matter altogether.

"It will be late when we reach the village," White Owl said after a long silence. "We'll sleep tonight, and you will meet my family tomorrow."

"That's good," Rose answered, relieved. The few things he had told her about his family had completely evaporated from her mind. Back then, she had been anxious to meet them. Now that their meeting was imminent, she was not nearly as excited. She clutched Molly's reins tighter in her sweating hands as White Owl led them into the quiet village.

Rose had seen Indian tepees before near the White River Agency. But the village at the edge of the agency was only about a third the size of White Owl's village. Rose was amazed to see hundreds of tepees crowded into this encampment. She fought back panic and glanced at White Owl for reassurance. He was staring straight ahead; his expression was tense. She swallowed hard and wiped away the perspiration on her brow.

The air was thick with a mixture of smells from campfire smoke to cooked meat, but all the fire pits were nothing more than cold ashes at this late hour. She was certain this had to do with the drought. It wouldn't be safe to go to bed and chance a stray spark starting a fire. Still, she was amazed that there was no activity in the village, because it couldn't be much past midnight. The howling of a lone dog somewhere in the distance was the only sound, until she heard coughing coming from one of the tepees. She held her breath until they had ridden past. She wasn't ready to face anyone yet.

As much as she wanted to be with White Owl, she was beginning to wonder whether she had made a mistake by insisting that he bring her to his village. She trusted White Owl with her life, but now she was among hundreds of other Utes who might not be as friendly toward a white woman. A sense of dread overcame her, but she straightened up in the saddle as she braced herself for whatever was waiting for her when the sun rose.

"This is my tepee," White Owl announced as he halted Niwaa at one of the many dwellings. "You can wait here, and I will take care of the horses."

"O-oh, all right," Rose stammered. He sounded so strange—so much like he regretted bringing her here. She climbed down from Molly's back and grabbed the leather satchel that held the few personal belongings she had brought with her. He grabbed the reins from her without further comment and led her horse away. She stood mutely in front of his tepee, watching him until both he and the horses had disappeared from her sight.

Unconsciously, she reached up to touch her gold heart necklace. She clutched at the bare skin at her neck . . . in her rush to leave the house earlier she must have forgotten to put it on. A deep sadness filled her at the realization that she had left her cherished memento behind.

Alone, the insecurities that she had been trying to avoid began to overcome her. She started to shake and she had to clench her teeth together to keep them from chattering. The temperature was probably seventy degrees, but she felt as though an icy wind had just engulfed her. Did White Owl feel forced to bring her here with him? Could that be why he was acting so strange now? Maybe he had been content to just see her at night to please his manly urges.

"Wild Rose." His voice sounded impatient. "Wild Rose," he repeated. "Are you coming in?"

Rose nodded. She had been so engrossed in her thoughts that she had not even heard him return. As he held the flap of the tepee open for her to enter, she ducked down and stepped inside. It was completely dark, and she could not make out any of her surroundings. She stood rooted to the spot, waiting and shivering, for him to tell her what to do.

When his hand grabbed hers in the darkness, she was so startled that she cried out in terror.

"What is wrong?" he asked as he pulled her close.

"I could ask you the same." Her voice was trembling and she had no doubt that he could feel how hard her entire body was shaky just by holding her hand.

"Why are you afraid?" His voice was softer now.

She took a deep, quivering breath. "Because it's obvious you don't really want me here."

He sighed loudly. But when Rose tried to draw her hand away, he pulled her up against him so suddenly that she gasped and dropped her satchel on the ground at her feet. She didn't have time to react as his strong arms encircled her upper body, pinning her own arms to her sides. A moment ago he couldn't even find words to say to her, and now, he was holding her so tightly that it felt like her ribs were being crushed.

"You don't know what I want," he whispered.

Rose could feel the heat of his breath against her hair. The trembling that had been in her whole body a moment ago now settled in her knees and she wasn't sure they could support her weight. "Tell me, then," she demanded.

"You. It's been you since that first day." He released his enslaving hold on her and leaned back slightly. "But I don't think you realize what you will be giving up to be with me."

"It doesn't matter," Rose answered. Her heart was thudding frantically in her breast again. All that mattered was that he still wanted her.

He shook his head hard enough that Rose was aware of it even in the darkness of the tepee. "Tomorrow it might matter. When the sun has risen and you have had time to think about your family, your life, all that you will be leaving behind if you should decide to stay with—"

"I know what I want, White Owl," she interrupted as she pulled away from him. "And if you want me, too, then nothing else matters."

His response was to pull her in his arms again. "We need to rest now," he said. "Tomorrow we will have many decisions to make."

"My decision is made," she retorted. She could feel his long hair brushing against the sides of her face as he leaned closer. She raked her hands through the raven strands. Almost immediately, he picked her up into his arms, carried her through the darkness and gently lay her down on a bed of furs. The soft bed smelled like him and filled her spinning senses with wanton needs that only this man could fulfill.

Tonight he made love to her only once, unlike the previous nights when they had been together in the loft at her parents' home. Those nights had been filled with a frantic passion that was fueled by the fear that they might never see each other again. Long before daylight broke, he would be gone and she would be back in her bedroom alone . . . waiting for the next night when, hopefully, he would return. But now, surrounded by his arms, in his world, she knew that when the sun rose over the mountain peaks they would be still be together.

More contented than she had ever felt in her entire life, Rose was held gently in his powerful embrace as she lay her head on her man's muscled chest and drifted off into a peaceful sleep.

Still tired from the lack of sleep for the past week, she could barely open her eyes when she felt White Owl's fingertips tenderly smoothing her hair back from her forehead. For a few moments she was too groggy to remember where she was, but she knew immediately whom she was with. As her heavy eyelids struggled to open, she thought momentarily that they were still in the loft and had accidentally fallen asleep. The thought that her father or one of her brothers might discover them caused her to wake fully with a start.

An early morning haze filtering through the smoke hole at the top of the tepee lit the interior with a mellow glow. She blinked and focused on White Owl's handsome face; his piercing dark gaze locked on hers. Her breath caught in her throat.

"Sorry. I did not mean to startle you," he said.

Rose ran her tongue along her lips and attempted to smile. The only thing that startled her was the way this man affected every one of her senses. Since she was still enveloped in his arms, it was obvious that neither of them had moved one inch from the other all night long. She was on her side, her naked body fully pressed against him and using his shoulder for a pillow. She marveled at his bronzed beauty in the soft rays of the morning light. His thick waist-length hair was spread out around him on the brown fur, framing his dark face and shoulders.

"You take my breath away," she finally gasped.

White Owl looked confused for a moment. "Am I that frightening in the morning?"

She giggled. "Not in a bad way." There was no way she could put into words how she was feeling at this moment. If waking up next to him every day like this was in her future, then she would never regret her decision to come here no matter what the consequences.

Even at this early hour, the heat was uncomfortable, and the interior of the animal-hide dwelling was growing hotter by the minute. But it wasn't only the temperature that was sweltering.

White Owl pushed the last of the stray hairs away from Rose's face and then lifted her chin up until she was in reach of his anxious lips. His good-morning kiss engulfed her mouth and every one of her senses. His lips were gentle at first, just barely touching hers. It was the only invitation Rose needed. She reached around his head and pulled herself on top of him and returned his teasing kiss with her own demanding one.

She felt his hands on her buttocks as he positioned her. Her hips moved on their own accord as he entered her. They fit together with perfection and began to move in a rhythm that was slow and sensuous at first, but began to build to a more intense summit as Rose sat up and let his swollen manhood fill her with sweet ecstasy. His hands held her by her hips as they moved with more urgency together, and just as Rose was feeling as if she was going to explode . . .

"White Owl, are you there?"

Rose's eyes flew open. She clapped her hand over her mouth to keep from crying out at the unexpected and shocking intrusion. Her gaze met with White Owl's, but he seemed more angry than surprised.

"What do you want?" he growled. He had not released his tight hold on Rose's hips.

"I heard noises, I—"

"Go away!" White Owl yelled. The fury in his voice was evident.

The building passion Rose had felt just seconds ago was now replaced with embarrassment.

White Owl's face was a mask of contempt as he glared toward the doorway of the tepee. Rose fully expected to drop dead of humiliation if that flap opened up and revealed their compromising position to the outside world.

"Sorry, my brother," the voice on the other side replied. A chortle followed and then silence . . . well, the voice was silenced anyway.

Now Rose became aware of all the sounds coming from outside this tiny haven that had sheltered her and White Owl. She could hear many different voices far and near. Obviously, the entire village was awake and—oh Lord! Had they been able to hear them? She had been so engrossed in passion just moments ago that she didn't even know if she had been crying out loud in sheer ecstasy. The thought made a very weak cry escape from her now.

White Owl's scowl began to fade, replaced by a crooked grin. Rose pushed against his chest as she rolled off his body. She heard him chuckle. Her mouth clamped shut. She was sure the entire village had already heard enough from her this morning. He chuckled again, and her ire increased.

Through clenched teeth, she whispered. "Be quiet before you have everyone in the village coming to see what is going on in here."

He rose up on one elbow and looked down at her. His hair fell over his muscled shoulders, and his raven gaze was sparkling like black diamonds. Rose was powerless to prevent the ache that erupted in her loins again. She clenched her legs together tightly and reached out to find something to cover herself with.

He laughed loudly now.

"You are insufferable!" she whispered in the most forceful voice she could manage. She sat up and presented her back to him, but before she could move away, his arms enslaved her waist, and he easily pulled her back to him. He kissed the back of her bare shoulder. Her insides turned to liquid fire. He pushed the long bulk of her hair over the other shoulder. His hot mouth continued to tantalize along the top of her shoulder, moving seductively to the back of her neck with tender kisses and teasing nips.

She moaned and rolled her head to the side so he could continue his delicious ministrations. One of his hands reached around and began to tease and fondle her breast. Sensations of unbridled desire rippled through her. Until this moment she had thought only the actual act of lovemaking could make her experience such glorious heights of satisfaction. Her body arched back against him, and she was flooded with desire. In spite of her vow to keep quiet, Rose could not contain a cry of delight.

White Owl's laughter disrupted the magical moment and brought her back to reality. Thankfully, he let her scoot away from him this time. She grabbed her nearest article of clothing—her white cotton pantaloons—and clutched them against her breast as she looked for the remainder of her clothes, which seemed to be scattered over the entire floor of the tepee.

"Are you ready to meet my family now?" White Owl asked innocently. He was grinning when she glanced back over her shoulder to cast him the most debasing look she could muster.

"You did that on purpose," she accused. "How can I show my face outside of this place after you made me practically scream out what we were doing?"

"I was only kissing your neck, Wild Rose."

"Only kissing and, and . . ." She started to rise to her feet to reclaim her clothes, but turned back around instead. "Close your eyes," she demanded.

He tossed back his head and gave a barrel laugh that caused Rose to twirl around and throw her hand over his mouth.

"Quiet!" she demanded through clenched teeth. She could still feel his entire body shaking with laughter. Finally, he choked back his mirth and pulled her hand away from his mouth.

"You are shy now, after all that we have done together?" He clamped his own hand over his mouth to cover his next chortle.

"That was different! Your entire family was not right outside the door." She narrowed her eyes and pursed her lips as she tried to convey just how serious she was.

His laughter slowly faded, but the smirk did not leave his mouth. He shook his head and glanced up at the ceiling. His arms were crossed over his broad chest as if he was forcing himself to hold still.

Rose glared at him for a moment longer to make sure he wasn't peeking. Then she rushed to gather her clothes and get dressed. She watched him the entire time. He had not moved, but the look of mirth on his face never faded, either.

"You can look now," she announced as she tried to untangle the knots in her hair with the hairbrush she had in her satchel. She stopped the useless task when she realized that he was staring at her. "What is it?" she asked, nervous.

He shook his head and smiled. "I've never seen you in the morning light before. You're even more beautiful, if that is possible."

His softly spoken words were like the sweetest music to Rose's ears. If she had ever doubted for one second whether she should have gone with him, that tiniest of doubt was now gone completely.

Chapter Fourteen

Rose was shaking so violently, she didn't think she would be able to speak. The thought of meeting White Owl's family and the other villagers had her terrified. She took White Owl's extended hand as he opened the flap and led her outside.

The village looked so different in the light of day. Now there were Indians everywhere. The air was heavy with smoke from the fires that cooked the morning meal, and there was activity wherever she looked: small children chased each other, dogs roamed around the fire pits looking for scraps of food to eat, and Rose found it impossible to believe that it was the same quiet dark village that she had entered the previous night.

Around the campfire nearest to White Owl's tepee, the conversation abruptly stopped. All eyes were focused on the couple who had just exited the tepee.

White Owl cleared his throat and pulled Rose up beside him. "This is Wild Rose," he said in a tone that sounded more like a command than an introduction. He wrapped his arm protectively around her waist and kept her pressed against his side.

Rose leaned as close to him as possible. She nodded her head numbly and glanced around, but all the faces blurred before her eyes. "H-hello," she finally managed to say.

The older man rose to his feet and approached her without hesitation. Rose knew immediately that he had to be White Owl's father. Although he had several long streaks of gray in his dark hair, he had the same regal, handsome features as White Owl. He smiled broadly and held out his hand to greet her.

"Hello, Wild Rose," he said in English that was almost as perfect as his son's.

Rose cast him a weak smile and held out her trembling hand.

"I am Strong Elk, father of White Owl," he said as he gave her hand one firm shake. He turned to the group that had gathered behind him and added, "This is my youngest son, Two Feathers." He motioned to the younger man who stepped up beside him. He did not offer his hand to Rose. She nodded her head toward him, but did not receive any acknowledgment. His dark stare did not look friendly, but she did not have time to contemplate his attitude.

A beautiful woman wearing a colorful full skirt and a loose-fitting white blouse stepped forward and smiled shyly. White Owl reached out and took the woman's hand. "Wild Rose, this is my mother, Sage."

Rose smiled back. She felt no animosity from

this woman, but she could tell by the way the woman was peering directly into her eyes that she was trying to determine if she was good enough for her son. "It is very nice to meet you," Rose said, hoping her voice conveyed sincerity.

The older woman nodded and backed away without speaking, but the expression on her lovely face seemed to be less critical.

Another younger woman stood beside White Owl's father. She did not smile or nod when White Owl introduced her. "That is Cloud Woman, my father's second wife."

Rose forced a smile, "Nice to meet you, too." She glanced at White Owl. A smirk curled one side of his mouth. He was obviously remembering her attitude about the Ute custom of having more than one wife. She raised one eyebrow in warning as their gazes met for an instant.

His taunting grin did not fade, but he looked away from her as he pointed to a young girl of possibly eleven or twelve. "That is Shy Girl," he said. "She is the daughter of my father and Cloud Woman."

"*Maiku*," the girl said quietly. "I mean, hello," she added in English. She glanced down at the ground, but a smile softly curved her full lips.

"Hello, Shy Girl," Rose said. The girl was thin and delicate, and obviously came by her name naturally. She was lovely, and Rose could see the family resemblance between her and White Owl.

A silence fell over the group after the last of the

introductions, until White Owl finally spoke up again. "Rose will be staying here with me. I have made her my woman."

His entire family stared at him. Rose was grateful that no one was looking at her because she knew her face had to be flaming red. He could have been more tactful, but no, he had just blurted it out, and now there was no telling how they would take her arrival.

The strained quiet did not last long—thanks to Strong Elk. "Rose, you sit here by me," he said as he motioned to a spot by the campfire. "I must learn more about the woman who has stolen my son's heart."

Rose was too stunned to move. If this had been her family, her father would probably have shot White Owl just for talking to her. But White Owl's father wanted her to sit beside him and chat as if they were old friends. Her head was spinning and she could not make her feet move.

"Rose?" White Owl said as he prodded her forward.

She thought the smirk appeared for an instant on his lips again, but if it did, it was gone immediately.

"You can tell my father how we met," he chided as he led her to the spot that Strong Elk had just motioned to.

She sank down on the hard ground. She was wearing a blue checked dress with a full skirt, so she crossed her legs like the rest of the group was doing and carefully tucked the material of the skirt around her legs. Nervously, she reached up to her neck and rubbed at the bare spot where her heart necklace should have been. She placed her hands back in her lap and clenched them tightly in an attempt to hide her uneasiness. As White Owl sat down next to her, she avoided looking at him. If he still wore that taunting grin, she would not be coherent enough to carry on a conversation with his father.

Strong Elk was staring at her when she glanced at him. She smiled timidly.

"Your dress is the same color as your eyes," he commented.

He stared directly into her eyes in a bold manner. Rose blinked several times and then lowered her gaze. She still avoided looking at White Owl, especially since she had heard him grunt when his father had made that comment.

"Rose could not keep those blue eyes off me when she first saw me," White Owl teased. "She rode many miles to watch me race my pony every day."

Rose turned to glare at him. "You've been doing quite a bit of riding lately to see me, too," she reminded him. She cast him a warning glance for an instant before she looked away from him again and directed her attention back to his father.

"I would like to thank you for making me feel so welcome," she said to Strong Elk. His smile was so similar to his oldest son's that Rose felt a tender tug at her heartstrings.

"You belong to my son, so now you belong to

my family." He held out a tin cup, and when she hesitated to take it, he said, "It is coffee from the agency."

"Thank you," she said sheepishly as she took the cup. It smelled strong, and the cup was almost so hot that she could not hold on to it. Although she put the cup up to her lips, she did not drink for fear of burning her tongue.

"How long will you stay?" the beautiful young girl named Shy Girl asked quietly.

Rose was surprised to hear the girl speak; she seemed so self-conscious. "I'm not sure," she answered. She glanced at White Owl out of the side of her eye.

"Forever, I hope," he replied.

His unexpected announcement caused an instant smile to light up Rose's face. She turned to look at him, and for a moment their gazes held, in spite of the curious crowd that watched them. By now a group of other villagers had begun to gather around them, obviously intrigued by Rose's presence. She ignored them as his sentiments echoed her internal dream . . . forever and ever.

White Owl smiled slightly, as if he knew exactly what she was thinking. Then he glanced back over his shoulder at the uninvited observers. He spoke in his Ute language. His tone sounded annoyed, and the group began to disperse immediately without making any comments.

Rose hoped his attitude would not make them angry with her. With a nervous glance back at his family, she noticed that none of them seemed to be overly worried about his words. Her eyes locked briefly with Two Feathers, however, and an ominous feeling gripped at her chest. His cold, penetrating stare seemed so filled with anger, or even hatred. Rose wrapped her arms around her body and quickly looked away.

The rest of the morning meal was uneventful. Rose nibbled at the flat bread Shy Girl had given to her and sipped the rest of the coffee once it was cool enough to drink. She did not look at Two Feathers again, but she liked Sage and Shy Girl more and more as the time wore on. They had both taken seats to her left so that they could visit with her, although the conversation did not involve anything more serious than the drought and the morning meal. Rose was amazed that everyone she had met so far spoke exceptionally good English. By the time they began to move away from the fire pit, her apprehension had faded . . . until she chanced another look at Two Feathers. He returned her glance with a cold smile, and his raven eyes still looked furious.

She leaned closer to White Owl. He immediately put his arm around her shoulders, oblivious to her fear. "They like you," he said as he smiled down at her. "Chief Jack will like you, too."

"Chief Jack?" She would ask White Owl about Two Feathers' strange behavior later.

"He is the leader of the younger Utes—the ones who are not going to let the whites take away our ponies or turn us into farmers." A mask of determination covered his face, but he quickly lost the serious attitude. "After we meet Chief Jack and explain why you are here, I will let my mother start teaching you the ways of Ute women."

"Oh," Rose answered in a timid tone. She glanced around at the women she could see and noticed that they were either clearing away the morning meal, tanning hides or chasing after small children. It did not appear that their daily routines were all that different than the way Rose and her mother spent their days. The men, on the other hand, were lying around doing nothing except visiting with one another and sipping their strong coffee. Several were curled up on the ground apparently sleeping again. Rose wondered if this was their usual morning routine. She knew that by midday the younger men would all be enjoying their favorite sport . . . horse racing in Powell Park.

Chief Jack, or Captain Jack, as he was sometimes called, was considered to be the last traditional chief of the Ute Indians, and the younger men of the tribe looked up to him as their leader because he refused to give in to the demands of the whites. Of course, Rose had no idea of this when she met him. He was almost as tall as White Owl and quite handsome. But still, not nearly as handsome as her warrior.

The chief greeted them with a raised hand as they approached his tepee. He was lounging on the ground against a pile of furs and motioned for them to join him. As Rose sat next to White Owl on the ground, she looked up and met the gaze of a young woman who sat close by working on a delicately beaded buckskin dress. Rose smiled, and to her relief, the other girl returned her friendly gesture. She appeared to be close to Rose's age, but whether she was Jack's wife was not clear.

Rose's attention was diverted when White Owl's warm hand surrounded her own hand. His smile was tender when she looked over at him and calmly announced, "Jack, meet my wife, Wild Rose."

His face blurred before her eyes as his words spun through her mind over and over again—"my wife." Was it true? Were they considered married in the laws of his tribe? Was she truly the wife of this powerful Ute warrior? It was not until she realized that Jack was congratulating them that she knew it was true.

"Thank you for your kind words," White Owl said as he squeezed Rose's hand and snapped her out of her shocked trance.

"Y-yes, thank you," Rose stammered. She had no idea what he had said to them. But White Owl was smiling widely, so she assumed that Chief Jack approved.

If only her own family could receive the news so joyfully. A sharp pain ripped through her breast. How could she ever tell her father face-to-face that she was now the wife of a Ute warrior? She gulped down the bitter taste in her mouth when she thought about what must have occurred at her parents' home this morning when they had found her note. But she refused to think about it now, because she did not want White Owl or Chief Jack to see her fall apart. She forced herself to concentrate on the present conversation.

White Owl's next statement sent Rose's senses into a tailspin. "We will be leaving soon for our wedding trip," White Owl said, then added something else in Ute.

Rose fought to control her emotions. She glanced back and forth between the chief and White Owl, but neither of them looked in her direction again.

Clearly they didn't want her to know what they were saying. Were they talking about the trouble brewing between the white settlers and the Utes? Even though she had heard her father talk about it, up until now the idea of there really being a war had not seemed possible.

Rose leaned into White Owl and felt his arm tighten around her. Her fear eased slightly. She had no doubt her new husband could protect her, but what about her family? Was there anything that could protect them?

Chapter Fifteen

"Are you all right?" White Owl asked as they left Chief Jack.

Rose nodded weakly. She was relieved that he had pulled her up to her feet, and she was still relying on him for support. Once she was certain they were far enough away, she whispered, "Please tell me your tribe is not going to start a war with the settlers?"

His body stiffened slightly. "Not with the settlers," he replied curtly. His arm was still wrapped around her waist and his steps lengthened. Rose practically had to run to keep up with him.

"With who, then?" Rose insisted. "Another tribe?" She held her breath as she waited for him to answer, although she was sure she didn't want to hear what he would say. A war with the people at the White River Indian Agency would only be the beginning, and the effect would result in a war with all the white men determined to chase the Utes out of the territory.

As they neared White Owl's tepee, he finally slowed his steps and stopped. He turned to look at Rose. His dark gaze was a window to his thoughts, and she was sure his torment was equal to her own. She closed her eyes for an instant and drew in a heavy breath. Before she could speak, White Owl pulled her up against his chest. She heard his heavy sigh whisper through her hair.

"I'm sorry, Wild Rose. Soon my people are going to fight with yours, and there is no way to stop it."

Rose felt a strangling fear rise up to her throat. She stepped back. "No!" The pain in his expression was obvious, but he could not offer her any comfort. "Please—no," she repeated.

"If you want to leave here—to return to your family—I will understand." His voice was low and raspy. "It will rip my heart out, but I will understand."

His words pushed all other thoughts from her mind. "I want to be with you forever," she said. "But my family . . ." She shook her head again, but could not clear away the image of her family being slaughtered if there should be a war.

White Owl tenderly pushed a stray curl back from her forehead. "Only the whites at the fort are in danger—because of Meeker. He is threatening to plow up our racetrack and kill our ponies. He says we have too many, but there is no such thing as too many ponies."

"Why? Why would he do that? Your horses and the track are such an important part of your lives."

"He does not understand our people. He thinks that we could be happy tending to crops all day, and he wants us to forget that we have been hunters since the beginning of time." He smiled tenderly and added, "Do not worry, my Wild Rose, your family is far away from the agency. They will be safe."

Rose exhaled heavily and tried to force a small smile. "I'll just hope that everything settles down and there is no war. I don't understand why we all can't live together in this beautiful country peacefully."

White Owl pulled her close and hugged her tightly. "That is just one of the many reasons I love you. If all whites could have a heart as kind as yours there would be no wars between our people."

She snuggled up against him as he held her in his arms. She wished she could put into words all the reasons she loved him. He represented everything that she wanted in a man. His passion for his people and this wondrous land; his kind and understanding nature; and most of all, their common belief that it did not matter whether someone was white or Indian. They were all human beings.

The sound of someone clearing their throat loudly interrupted their tender moment. Two Feathers said something in the Ute language that Rose did not understand. He looked only at White Owl as he spoke.

White Owl nodded, but did not say anything back to his younger brother. As Two Feathers turned and stalked away, White Owl glanced back down at Rose.

"My father wants to talk to me," he said.

Rose nodded, but she desperately wanted to ask

about Two Feathers' hostile behavior toward her. She held her questions for now, however, because she didn't want to anger Strong Elk by making him wait for White Owl. As they made their way back to Strong Elk's tepee, Rose could not help worrying about Two Feathers' attitude. She would have to work extra hard to befriend him, since it was obvious that he did not approve of this marriage. Marriage!

That one word erased all Rose's previous worries. It still didn't seem real to her without an actual ceremony, but since the Utes were considered married just by sleeping with the one they chose, then she and White Owl were definitely married. She felt her cheeks grow hot just with the thought of their passionate nights over the past few weeks.

She was still lost to those sensual memories when they arrived at Strong Elk's lodge. The thought that she was now officially married to White Owl and was going to spend every night in his arms was overruling all other thought.

"Come, sit here with me," Sage said to Rose, patting the ground next to her. Spread out in front of her was a beautiful piece of material that had diagonal stripes every color in the rainbow.

As Rose sat next to the woman, Shy Girl rushed over to sit next to her. "*Maiku*," she said as a broad smile curved her lips. "Hello."

"*Maiku* to you," Rose returned. She thought she might as well start learning the language, even if it did seem that everyone she had met so far spoke

English. She glanced up and saw White Owl and his father walking away from the group. They were speaking low, and she was not able to hear their conversation. Rose swallowed hard.

"I am making new skirt," Sage announced. She used a knife to cut through the material as expertly as most people used a pair of scissors.

"It is lovely material," Rose answered as she forced her attention away from White Owl and his father. They had disappeared from view. Obviously, they did not want anyone else to hear their conversation. A sharp pain shot through Rose's breast.

"You should make it for Wild Rose," Shy Girl suggested.

"Oh," Rose gasped as she realized what Shy Girl had just said. "No, I couldn't. I mean, that is such a nice thought, Shy Girl, but much too generous." She reached out and squeezed the girl's hand affectionately, adding, "She should make something for you. That material is beautiful, just like you."

The young girl blushed, and as she glanced down toward the ground, a huge smile curved her full lips.

Rose glanced up and met Sage's gaze. They exchanged smiles but not words. A sense of belonging settled in Rose, until she thought of her own mother. Thinking of what she was probably going through made Rose feel sick to her stomach. She could only pray that her father would not take out his rage on the rest of her family.

Rose tried to focus on the task Sage was doing,

because she could feel the threat of tears in her eyes. The guilt of running away was overwhelming, but she did not regret what she'd done.

If she had stayed, she would be leaving for Denver right now. She would be leaving White Owl. That was not an option. As she choked down the heavy lump in her throat and wiped angrily at the unwanted tears, a gentle hand was placed on her arm.

"You sad?" Sage asked in a worried tone.

Rose attempted a feeble smile. "Not sad to be here. But my mother, she will be so worried about me. I hope she will forgive me someday."

Sage put down the knife she had been cutting the material with and scooted closer to Rose. She put a comforting arm around Rose's shoulders. "When she sees you so happy with White Owl, she forgive," Sage said softly.

Rose nodded and wiped at the tears rolling down her cheeks. "Yes—you're right—she will, but my father, he-he—," Rose could not even begin to think about her father's reactions.

Sage hugged her tighter. "Fathers are scared for their girls. Someday he understand."

"I hope you're right." Her father's furious face flashed before her eyes, and his hate-filled words about the Utes flooded her mind. Fear clutched at her insides. She could not fathom that he would ever understand the path that she had chosen for her life.

She realized that Shy Girl was on her other side and was rubbing her back in a sympathetic gesture. A worried frown drew her lips down, and her thick dark brows were drawn closely together as if she was feeling Rose's pain. Rose reached over and patted the younger girl's arm as their gazes met briefly. The maturity that she saw in the girl's solemn gaze surprised her.

"Would you like to try?" Sage said to change the subject. She held the knife out for Rose and motioned toward the material. "I think Shy Girl would like a new skirt."

Just as Rose took the knife from Sage, an angry female voice rang out from the tepee. Rose jumped at the sound, although she could not understand what Cloud Woman was saying because she spoke in Ute. Shy Girl, however, appeared to be the person she was addressing. The younger girl jumped to her feet at once and walked quickly into the tepee.

"Is she in trouble for talking to me?" Rose asked. It was becoming obvious that not everyone was happy to have her here.

Sage shrugged but did not have time to answer. White Owl and his father were walking toward them, and White Owl's full attention was focused on his bride. Rose's gaze met his twinkling dark eyes at once; he looked more than a little excited about something.

"Are you ready to begin your life as my wife?" he asked as one side of his mouth lifted in a suggestive smirk.

"I-I thought we already had—" Rose clamped her mouth shut as she felt a scorching blaze race through her entire body and ignite a fire in her cheeks. Had she really said that in front of his parents? Her mortification intensified when she saw the way White Owl's brows raised up in surprise. His smirk immediately became a full-fledged smile.

"Our wedding trip will make it legal."

"Oh, good," Rose replied. Her voice was barely more than a hoarse whisper. She could not bring herself to look at Sage or at Strong Elk. Even though the Ute culture was obviously drastically different from what she was accustomed to, talking about intimate activities that she and White Owl engaged in was not something she wanted to divulge.

"Let's go now," White Owl added. His voice sounded excited and anxious. "I'll grab your bag and our bedding." He disappeared into the tepee.

Even though she could still feel the blush burning in her face, Rose forced herself to look at Sage as she handed the knife back to her. To her amazement, the older woman was smiling proudly at the tepee where her oldest son had just disappeared through the hide flap. Sage looked back at Rose as she took the knife and added, "My heart soars because you make my son so happy."

A timid grin touched Rose's lips. "Thank you." She didn't have time to say anything else because White Owl was emerging from the tepee with her leather satchel and an armful of other supplies and furs.

"She makes me happier than you know," he replied to his mother. His expression was tender and his dark eyes sincere as he gazed back toward Rose.

A tremor of excitement raced through her as she rose to stand beside her husband. She hoped this feeling would never go away.

White Owl waved at his mother as he began to lead Rose away.

Rose glanced back at Sage. "Good-bye . . . and thank you for your kindness." The other woman's face lit up with happiness as she waved good-bye to Rose. A tender smile rested on her lips. Rose thought about her own mother again. When they returned from their trip, she would go back long enough to apologize to her for the way she had left. But until then, she did not intend to allow any sad thoughts to intrude on the joy that she was feeling as the wife of her handsome Ute warrior.

As they made their way to the edge of the village where Molly and Niwaa waited for them, Rose felt many eyes focused in their direction. She concentrated on staring straight ahead and keeping up with White Owl's long strides. He seemed completely unaffected by the attention they were attracting, and if possible, he seemed even more anxious than she was to begin their honeymoon— or wedding trip, as he referred to it.

When they reached the horses, Rose was surprised to see that Molly stood saddled and ready next to Niwaa.

"I was getting the ponies ready while you were getting to know my mother," he said with a smug smile. He placed her bag over the back of her saddle and then went to secure the supplies and blankets he had brought behind his saddle.

When he was finished organizing the large load, White Owl grasped her around the waist, effortlessly lifted her up onto Molly's back, and handed her the reins without saying a word. He appeared so eager, Rose began to wonder just what a Ute wedding trip entailed. There was absolutely no way the passion they already shared could improve, was there? A powerful shiver shook her body. She grasped the reins tighter and glanced at White Owl. He was watching her curiously. A grin curved his mouth, and he nodded his head as if he knew exactly what she was thinking. Rose drew in a sharp breath and gently kicked Molly in the sides to urge her forward.

Rose giggled. "You sure wasted no time in arranging this trip. Are we in a hurry or something?"

He shrugged. "Do you have something you'd rather be doing?" One dark brow lifted in a curious arch above his right eye.

Rose's mind went blank, and the now familiar ache started turning her insides to a mass of yearnings. She could barely manage to shake her head.

A grin claimed White Owl's mouth again. His chest puffed out slightly, and he strode to his horse and swung up on its back in one graceful bound. Rose swallowed hard. She hoped their destination was not very far.

Chapter Sixteen

After the first hours that they had traveled, Rose could not help being disappointed. Instead of riding through the lush pines and aspens that surrounded the Ute lands and Milk Creek, they headed straight north into country that was miles and miles of nothing more than sagebrush and small rolling hills. She had envisioned them spending their wedding trip at some mountain hideout surrounded by trees and deep blue lakes. Now, it seemed, they were headed directly for the desert.

Since Rose had no intention of questioning White Owl about their destination, she tried to focus on looking around the barren countryside, and before long, she began to realize that it represented a different kind of beauty than the mountainous regions offered. The end of summer, and the long drought, had turned most of the surrounding landscape to shades of brown and tan, with a few scattered patches of green foliage on an occasional bush here and there. But it was the distant vista that was breathtaking. Rose drank in the views of the faraway mountains bathed in a misty blue hue from the azure sky. The various peaks were sharp in some areas and rounded in others, forming a majestic skyline; they appeared almost mystical and unreal. They seemed another world away, but they appeared to be riding toward them.

Since the afternoon had grown hot, and riding was uncomfortable, Rose was grateful when White Owl suggested that they rest until it cooled down. "How much farther?" she asked as they spread a woven blanket in the shade of an old gnarled oak tree.

"We should be there in two days' time."

"Two days!" Rose retorted. "Why are we going so far?"

"I am taking you to a place that is very special to me."

"Oh," Rose answered quietly. His voice had sounded strange, almost as if she had hurt his feelings. "If it is special to you, then I know I will love it," she added.

He had lowered himself to the ground and was reclining on his side. When he patted the spot next to him on the blanket, Rose did not wait for another invitation. She settled against his body as comfortably as if he was merely an extension of her. With her head resting on his bare chest, Rose's fingers traced the taut muscles of his stomach and chest. She heard him sigh softly and then felt his lips tenderly kiss the top of her head. She let her eyes close as he gently ran his fingers through her hair. The sense of peace she felt in his arms washed over her immediately, and combined with the heat of the day, drowsiness overpowered the passion she had been feeling a moment earlier.

Rose opened her eyes slowly when she felt a large hand shaking her gently.

"Beautiful," White Owl whispered as she focused on his face hovering above her.

"What's beautiful?" she asked in a groggy voice.

"My new wife."

"That sounds so"—Rose sighed—"nice." It still did not seem possible that she was actually married to a Ute warrior, but in her mind, he was only the man that she loved, and nothing else mattered.

"We should try to ride farther now that the sun is not so hot," White Owl said. He glanced up at the sun, hanging low on the western horizon.

Rose sat up and rubbed her eyes. "It's already late. Maybe we should just stay here tonight." She intentionally raised one brow in a suggestive arch like he always did to her—a gesture that did not go unnoticed.

White Owl shook his head as a teasing smile curved his mouth. "Could it be that my wife enjoys lying with me? Most Ute women usually act like it is their obligation."

Rose quickly wiped the smile from her face. A heated sensation rushed through her face. He must think that she was insatiable. When his roar of laughter broke in to her moment of embarrassment, anger began to join the rest of her raging emotions.

"That is not a bad thing, Wild Rose!" He smacked his hand against his chest, adding, "I am proud to know that I make my wife happy."

Rose scooted closer to him and replaced her pout with another smile. "You should be a very, very proud man then, if that is the case." She rose up to his lips with a tender kiss.

White Owl leaned back on his heels and sighed. "We need to go now."

Rose let out a disappointed groan. "What is the hurry? We have the rest of our lives together." A strange expression passed across White Owl's face. "What is it?" she asked, alarmed.

A smile replaced his strange look. "Nothing, except I'm just eager to show you my special place." He rose to his feet and pulled Rose up with him, but he made no attempt to explain further. He wrapped his arm around her waist and led her to the horses.

Rose studied his face as he readied the animals for riding, but he gave no hint of the odd expression she had noticed a few seconds earlier. One thing she was certain of, however, he was determined to get to their destination as quickly as possible.

They continued toward the mountains and did not stop until the land was bathed in complete darkness. They spread their bedrolls under a sprawling clump of cedars and snuggled together to ward off the slight chill of the night. Since they were both too tired to do much more than kiss good night, they slept through the night until the faint glow of the rising sun woke them. Before they continued on their journey, they made slow, passionate love, relishing in the realization that they no longer had to sneak around in the barn at Rose's parents' ranch or worry about being overheard by the villagers at White Owl's camp. Their desire had no limitations now.

"I want to start every day for the rest of my life just like this," Rose sighed. White Owl's sigh echoed her own, but he did not speak. He pulled her as close as was humanly possible as they snuggled under the blanket and allowed their fevered bodies to calm from the impassioned lovemaking they had just engaged in. Rose closed her eyes and sighed again. There really were no words she could use to describe this feeling of overwhelming love that she felt for this man.

"We should go now, before the day grows hot."

Rose sighed again, but with much less contentment. Although she cherished this time alone with her new husband, his quest to travel so far for their wedding trip seemed unnecessary. But she would gladly follow him to the ends of the earth, so she pushed her weary body up from the ground.

Their second full day of traveling was uneventful, but felt extremely long to Rose. Her butt hurt, and her back ached; in fact, all of her body hurt. Although they stopped frequently to water the horses, she began to worry about Molly, since the little mare was not accustomed to being ridden this long. When she mentioned this to White Owl, he brushed off her worries.

"Ponies are meant to be ridden, Wild Rose. That is why the Great Spirit created magic dogs."

"Great Spirit?"

"The Ute god," White Owl answered. "I noticed right away how good you were to your pony. That was one of the first things I loved about you."

Rose smiled. "Utes call their horses magic dogs?"

"Sometimes. It's just an old expression." He motioned for her to mount again. "We're never going to get there if we keep talking." One dark brow arched suggestively.

Rose wasted no time in pulling herself onto Molly's back. Any amount of discomfort was worth the end result, which she was looking forward to with more than a little enthusiasm.

They stopped again during the heat of the day, but neither Rose nor White Owl was able to fall asleep, and once they started riding again, Rose felt so weary she was afraid she would fall off Molly's back.

They made camp before dark beside a little stream that ran along the base of a cedar-covered hill. The setting sun bathed the entire area in a golden glow. They washed in the brook, and Rose felt much more refreshed. Once they had eaten a quick meal of corn cakes and coffee, then spread out the furs and blankets, it was only a matter of minutes before they were wrapped in each other's arms. Exhausted from riding and from the heat of the day, they were both asleep just minutes after lying down.

"We will reach Vermillion Basin today," White Owl said as the sun rose the next morning.

Rose's attention was riveted by the contrast between the hues of their skin, with the rising sun spotlighting his pale brown skin against her nearly alabaster skin tone. She wondered how hard it would always be for them in this world that was so filled with prejudice and hate.

"What's wrong?" White Owl asked.

"Nothing," Rose lied. "Why?"

"You grew so tense and you shook. Are you cold?"

Rose swallowed hard. She told herself her love for White Owl would see them through the hardships they would undoubtedly face because of their differences. "Maybe a little cold, and really dreading riding again today. I wish we didn't have to move." She snuggled as close as possible to the muscled body of her husband. His arms immediately tightened around her. She definitely had not been lying about dreading the ride again today.

"How will you survive the winter if you think it is cold now?" White Owl asked with a chuckle.

"You will keep me warm," Rose replied. She pushed away the worries she had been dwelling on regarding their future and concentrated on their beautiful surroundings. They had woken in a valley of cedars, and the heady pine scent emitting from their branches was intoxicating.

"Tell me more about this special place we are going," she asked in an effort to divert her thoughts to the present.

"You will see it soon."

Rose gave up asking questions, since it was obvious she wasn't going to get any answers. Luckily, she did not have long to wait until they reached their destination.

As they rode into a tall narrow canyon that couldn't have been more than thirty feet wide, Rose was in awe of the towering rock walls in various shades of brown, rust and tan-colored sandstone. She gasped when she saw pictures of people and animals etched into some of the rugged rocks overhead. White Owl heard her and chuckled as he pointed to the scattering of detailed pictures.

"My ancestors came here many, many moons ago and drew pictures on the rocks so that we could be reminded of our great beginnings." He halted his horse and gestured toward a large picture of an Indian wearing an elaborate headdress and holding a bow in his hand. The rock that the picture was carved into was at least fifty feet high, yet the details were intricate.

"They are so beautiful," Rose said in amazement. "How did they ever get up there to do that?"

White Owl shrugged. "I told you this place is special." At a later time, he would show her the remnants of a tattered bark and vine ladder that those first people who lived here had used to scale the cliff walls. Even with the primitive ladder, etching the pictures in the stone had been a remarkable task. He nudged his horse forward, but kept the pace slow so that they could observe more of the numerous pictures of animals, people and assorted weapons that covered the cliffs and high rocks.

Rose followed him on her horse, her gaze flitting from one side to the other of the towering canyon walls. She could not even begin to imagine how the Indians had scaled those steep rocks, let alone dangled out there in front of them long enough to etch those massive pictures in the hard stone. White Owl had been right . . . it was worth traveling this far to see this mystical place, and she sensed that this was only the beginning of the surprises her handsome husband had in store for her.

As they rode out of the breathtaking canyon, the area opened up to expose a secluded meadow surrounded by pinyons, cedars, and sagebrush. To Rose, it looked like they had entered their own private world, but a huge round rock fire pit was built smack in the center, reminding her that other people had been here before them. A sense of admiration overtook her as she stopped her horse beside White Owl's. "It's truly magical," Rose said quietly.

"My grandfather brought me here several times when I was small. It was like a magic place to me, too. After he died, I came here once on my own, but it was not the same. When I first met you, I knew that I would bring you here someday." He turned to look at her, adding, "And now, the magic has returned."

Rose swallowed the lump that had formed in her throat as she met her husband's loving gaze. "Thank you for bringing me here."

White Owl drew a deep breath but did not reply

immediately. His tender expression exposed his thoughts. After a moment of silence, he finally asked, "Would you like to see your new home?"

Rose nodded with enthusiasm as he dismounted, and then he helped her down from her horse. He took her hand and began to lead her back toward the canyon, but before they entered the narrow opening, they turned and began to hike up a rocky slope that led to a ledge several hundred feet above. The rocks almost seemed to create a natural stairway and the climb was easy. Within minutes they were standing on the ledge.

"Oh," Rose gasped as she looked at the cave that had been completely hidden from the valley below.

The ledge cut into the rock and was approximately thirty feet long. An overhanging rock created a roof over almost the entire area. Cut deep into the back of the ledge was a huge cave with a rock fire pit in the center. Rose pulled White Owl with her as she stepped into the cave. Although they had to duck slightly to enter under the overhanging rock ceiling, once they were inside, even White Owl could stand upright with several inches to spare overhead.

"It's perfect," she whispered. "Can we stay here forever?"

White Owl chuckled. "Would you not get lonely?"

Rose turned to him. "I will never be lonely as long as I am with you." She glanced around the cave, wondering where they would put their bed.

As if White Owl was reading her mind, he cleared his throat loudly and turned back toward the opening. "Let's get the supplies."

With an eager nod, Rose followed him back out of the cave. She stopped at the edge of the rock ledge and looked around. Below her was the hidden meadow and to her right was the entrance into the deep rugged canyon with the ancient carvings. In the distance, she could see the tops of towering mountains that had seemed so far away just a couple of days ago. Rose felt her breath catch in her throat. It was awe inspiring, and she felt blessed just to be standing here.

"Come," White Owl called out. "We will explore later."

Rose snapped out of her trance and hurried down the slope to help her husband with their gear. She was eager to explore, but even more eager to get their soft furs spread out in the cave.

With her arms loaded, she carefully made her way back up the slope and deposited the furs and blankets inside the cave, while White Owl concentrated on setting up camp around the big fire pit in the meadow. She studied the inside of the cave carefully and finally determined that she would make the bed in the narrowest corner of the cave. She had to bend down slightly as she spread the thick furs out, because this corner sloped and was a little lower in height than the rest of the cave. But when she finished smoothing out the last of the blankets over the furs and stood back to admire her work, she felt that it was the perfect place for their bed. A chuckle distracted her as White Owl entered the cave.

"That is where I used to put my bed when I came here with my grandfather. I was shorter then and didn't even have to bend over to smooth the furs."

"Oh, do you mind that you will have to bend down now to—" Her words were cut off when her husband grabbed her arm and twirled her around. His mouth descended on hers with a demanding kiss. Rose decided he didn't mind as she returned his kiss with her own demands. She reached up and encircled his neck with her arms, drawing herself up against him as close as possible. His engorged manhood pressed into her abdomen and her knees went weak.

White Owl swept her into his arms and walked the several steps to the newly made bed. He bent down easily with her and placed her on top of the soft bed. As he lowered himself on her, Rose immersed her fingers in his long hair. The feel of his thick, heavy hair in between her fingers was always like an aphrodisiac to her, and she arched up against him, insatiable for all of him. Her greediness was appeased.

They pulled apart only long enough to disrobe, and when their bodies came together again, there was nothing but heated flesh and building desire between them. White Owl wasted no time in entering her with an urgency that seemed almost out of control. Their bodies moved as one, and each demanding plunge caused Rose's passion to increase until she felt as if she was going to implode from within. His wet kisses claimed her labored breaths as this impassioned ritual reached a climax.

White Owl shuddered as his zealous movements came to a halt, and his mouth kissed Rose's swollen lips one more time before he rolled to her side. He hugged her tightly against his sweating body as they both allowed themselves to ease back down from this lofty summit.

Rose ran her fingertips down the muscled, sweaty expanse of White Owl's hard stomach and gently encircled his belly button as she let her fingers travel lower. White Owl moaned. His response was immediate as he pulled her up on top of him and placed her precisely on his swollen member. His large hands held her buttocks firmly as he began to move within her again. A weak cry escaped from Rose as she splayed her hands across the sinewy muscles of his smooth chest and began to move her hips with his, meeting each one of his urgent thrusts with her own demands.

She arched back when his hands grasped ahold of her breasts and his fingers began to fondle the protruding nipples. A guttural cry escaped her. She had known ecstasy with him each time they had made love, but none of those other times could even begin to compare to the times they made love in this position. His deep penetration created a delicious pain that flooded through her, and the way his fingers always tantalized her breasts at the same time drove every inch of her—inside and out—crazy with brazen desires. She wondered how many other positions they had not explored yet.

The hidden cave on the craggy sandstone bluff was filled with their love; their first home as man and wife had been initiated, and their wedding trip was finally beginning.

Chapter Seventeen

Vermillion Creek was no more than a trickle of water struggling to cut a tiny path through the hard ground because of the long months of drought. There was a small pond where they could get some water for cooking and washing, but Rose and White Owl had to make a trip farther west to the Green River to get fresh drinking water. It was an easy trip since there was not anything other than sagebrush and a cluster of pinyon or scraggly cedars here and there between Vermillion Basin and the river.

They followed a wide valley most of the way and by the time they had reached the river, it was late afternoon. The setting sun cast purple and blue shadows on the smooth rocks along the river's edge. It was barely the beginning of September, but already the leaves on the scrub oaks were starting to turn into an array of orange and gold. The afternoon heat, however, felt more like mid-July.

"Here is a good spot," White Owl said as he halted Niwaa beside the river.

It had been a long, hot ride, and the smooth cool waters of the river were mighty inviting. Almost instantaneously they both jumped down from their horses and ran, laughing, toward the river. Rose began undoing the little cloth-covered buttons that ran down the front of her white blouse the second she noticed that White Owl was kicking off his moccasins and rolling his leggings down. Since she had on considerably more clothes than he did, Rose was forced to stop at the edge of the river to finish removing her long flowered skirt.

White Owl had not stopped and plunged into the deep green water. His body made a loud splash, and when he resurfaced he let out a war whoop.

Rose laughed as she was sprayed with water from his jump. She threw off her tan hat and kicked off her tall riding boots and stepped forward to jump in with him.

"All of it," White Owl demanded.

"What?" Rose asked as she teetered on the edge of the riverbank. She realized White Owl was pointing at the undergarments she'd left on.

She clutched the front of her cotton camisole tightly. "But someone could ride up," she protested.

"I will come up there and take them off for you," White Owl replied with a sly grin.

Rose closed her eyes for an instant and shook her head in defeat. She opened her eyes again, half expecting to see White Owl climbing out of the water to make good on his threat. But he had not moved and was watching her with a look that did nothing to hide his sensuous thoughts. Rose's breath stopped short as she met his intense gaze. With his raven hair floating around him in the dark green water and his wet skin glistening over his broad, muscled shoulders and chest, he appeared almost spiritual. He was constantly telling her that he could not deny her anything, but now she realized it went both ways. There was nothing she could deny him either.

Slowly Rose reached behind her head and pulled the ribbon from her hair, releasing the ponytail and sending her long hair spilling down her back. Next she began to untie the little satin bow at the top of her camisole and undo the tiny buttons that ran down the front. She pushed one side of the garment off from one shoulder—and then the other side—and let it fall from her back.

White Owl did not move, his eyes burning into her hot flesh. She pushed the pantaloons down over her flat stomach and the curve of her hips. As they slid down her thighs and past her knees, she stepped out of them. She was certain she heard him gasp, but she kept her eyes locked with his, because she knew if she looked anywhere else, she would die of embarrassment.

White Owl held his breath as he watched his beautiful young wife strip her clothes away. Her hair shimmered around her bare skin like a profusion of deep red flames. He let his gaze travel leisurely over her body. Her long legs were slender and perfectly shaped. The sight of her standing on the riverbank made his manhood rise up in the water and ache without mercy.

He was transfixed as she shook her wavy hair

out around her shoulders and started to step to the edge of the riverbank. She bent forward and dove into the water, landing just a few feet in front of him. White Owl blinked to clear the water from his eyes. His blurry vision cleared just in time to see her emerge from under the water. Her eyes were closed, and the tips of her long lashes had tiny droplets of water teetering on the edges. She reached up and brushed the water away from her eyes and then smoothed the hair back away from her face. Her eyes opened, and their blue gaze immediately settled on him. White Owl exhaled the breath he had been holding in one huge gush.

Within a second she was in his arms and their slick wet skin was melded together. White Owl claimed her lips with a kiss that was hard and filled with urgency. Their tongues entwined, and he could taste her natural sweetness mixed with the unique taste of the river water. He picked her up around the waist and felt those shapely, long legs wrap around his hips as he entered her with an excitement that he couldn't contain any longer.

Being in the water was a whole new sensation, and it wasn't long before they both reached their climax. With her legs still around his hips, he waded toward the edge of the river, then gently, reverently washed her body as they reclined in a shallow pool along the riverbed.

Hunger eventually drew them from the water. Rose started a campfire, while White Owl went back to the water to catch a fish for dinner.

Under the star-studded Colorado sky, they bedded down for the night. White Owl held his wife tightly in his embrace while he listened to her soft breaths as she slept. He could not get the images out of his mind of her standing nude and glorious on the riverbank or the way she had looked when she had emerged from the water. He was certain there had never been a goddess in all of history— Ute or white—who could compare with her.

He had always known he would claim a wife someday, but he had not been in a hurry to do so. Marriage had only seemed like a requirement for a man, regardless of whether he loved the woman. If he enjoyed her lovemaking, that was usually enough. So, if only a few weeks ago, someone had told him that he would be so ferociously in love— with any woman—White Owl would have called them a liar. But now he couldn't begin to imagine a future without his Wild Rose. He only wished they would never have to return to a life that would constantly try to test their unending love.

Chapter Eighteen

Rose gingerly sipped the scalding coffee from the tin cup she held in both hands. This morning was the first time it had actually felt like an autumn day. The long drought seemed as though it was about to come to a screeching halt by the way the darkening clouds were gathering overhead. She had no idea how long they planned to stay in this enchanting place—White Owl just shrugged whenever she asked him, but she had a feeling he did not intend to linger through the winter months.

She guessed that they had been here nearly two months, but time meant nothing here. Although she knew it was not feasible, she really did wish they could stay forever. Spending the rest of her life alone with her virile and handsome husband, completely secluded from the rest of the world, did not sound bad at all.

The sound of horse hooves snapped Rose out of her wishful daydreaming. White Owl had ridden out earlier to hunt in case the weather turned severe and they had to hole up in their cozy cave for a few days, an idea that sounded very appealing to

Rose. She smiled to herself as she placed her coffee cup on the ground and rose to her feet.

As the rider drew closer, however, Rose realized that he was not her beloved husband. It was a Ute, though; she could see the colorful striped wool coat he wore over his tan leggings. But a flat-topped, wide-brimmed black hat hid his face. She wrapped her woolen blanket tighter around her body as she felt a sudden chill that had nothing to do with the cooler weather.

Only when the rider was a few feet away could she tell it was Two Feathers. The knowledge did not ease her mind.

He stared down at her, unspeaking, for a moment and then glanced around the campsite. "Where is my brother?" His chiseled expression and the coldness in his tone only served to increase Rose's fear.

"H-he is hunting," she stammered. Her feet were rooted to the spot, even as he climbed down from his horse and walked to the opposite side of the fire pit to warm his hands.

"He will be happy to see you," Rose finally managed to say. Her feeling of dread increased when his only reply was a grunt.

She motioned toward the tin pan on one of the rocks that ringed the fire. "Would you like coffee?"

A quick nod was Two Feathers' response.

As she got another cup and poured the coffee, she could sense his hostile stare watching her every move. By the time she reached out to give him the cup, her hands were shaking. His cold fingertips briefly touched her hand. He grabbed the cup and pulled back as if he had been stung by a bee. She glanced up and met his gaze; the hatred that he felt toward her radiated from his narrowed black eyes. Rose backed away so quickly that she tripped over the long blanket still wrapped around her shoulders. She would have fallen if a pair of strong hands had not grabbed her and stopped her from hitting the ground.

White Owl steadied her. The look on his face was pained and filled with confusion.

"I did not hear you ride up," Rose said as she tried to regain her composure.

"I let Niwaa loose down at the creek." White Owl turned away from her. "My brother, it is good to see you. I hope you did not bring bad news?"

Two Feathers met his brother's gaze. "No, no bad news. All is good."

Rose heard White Owl exhale as if he was relieved. "Then you come because you miss your big brother," White Owl replied as he attempted to sound jovial.

They had been together long enough that Rose was becoming attuned to her husband's moods and the tones of his voice. She knew now that his words were only that . . . words, and there was a much deeper meaning to Two Feathers' arrival.

"Our father and mother miss you. But I am glad you are gone." Two Feathers' attempt to joke was not conveyed in his expression. He took another swig from the coffee cup. "I can see that there is no need to worry, my brother. You look well."

White Owl's arm encircled Rose's shoulder as he pulled her against him. "Yes, my wife keeps me very happy." He smiled down at her.

Rose swallowed the heavy lump in her throat. She could not speak. In spite of her husband's comforting hold, she did not feel safe. She glanced at Two Feathers. His expression was the same: unreadable and distant.

White Owl loosened his hold on Rose. "I have brought back a rabbit to eat." He motioned toward the kill lying at his feet. "Wild Rose will cook it for us."

Rose nodded and quickly moved to retrieve the dead rabbit. She was anxious to move away from Two Feathers. Besides, it was obvious that the real reason for his visit would not be discussed until she was out of earshot. Still, she was more than a little curious to know why he had showed up so unexpectedly. Someday she also hoped to learn why he hated her so much.

As Rose cleaned the rabbit, she strained to hear the conversation between her husband and his brother. But they had walked away from the camp and she could hear nothing but the howling wind bellowing through the valley. The flames in the big fire pit danced beneath the pot Rose had hung from a spit above the fire. Soon they would have to start cooking at the fire pit in the cave, instead of out here in the meadow. Rose attempted to keep her blanket wrapped tightly around her shoulders as she placed the rabbit in a pot over the fire to boil for rabbit stew.

She glanced up as she heard the men approaching. Neither of them met her gaze. Rose shivered more violently and wrapped her arms tightly around herself. However, she was more nervous than she was cold.

"Wild Rose is becoming a good cook," White Owl said in a tone that was more enthusiastic than necessary.

A grunt was Two Feathers' reply.

"Thank you, husband," Rose said as she bent to stir the contents in the pot. The water was just beginning to come to a boil. Yesterday, when White Owl had predicted that the weather was going to turn cold, they had spent the day gathering up the roots and autumn berries before the freeze. Now she tossed a portion of those edible fruits and vegetables into the pot. The majority of them were in the cave drying so that they could store them for later on.

She glanced back up and unintentionally met the surly stare of her brother-in-law. Her gaze dropped to the ground, and as she took a clumsy step backward, she once again tripped over the long tip of the blanket. But this time, White Owl was not close enough to catch her. Her fall seemed slow moving as she began to tumble forward. But when she was grabbed roughly and placed upright on her feet again, she had not even had time to take a complete breath. A gasp escaped from her as she looked up into the hateful glare of her rescuer. Two Feathers' expression did nothing to induce her gratitude.

"You should be careful—you could have a bad accident," Two Feathers said flatly.

Rose felt the strong arms of her husband surround her. "Are you all right?" he asked. "I think you need to get rid of that blanket."

Rose ran her tongue along her dry lips. "Yes, I will get my coat. And thank you, Two Feathers." Her voice was hoarse and her breath felt as if it was not reaching her lungs. Her rescuer did not respond to her words of appreciation.

White Owl kept her in his tight embrace and Rose leaned against him as closely as possible. Two Feathers' unfriendly glare made her feel vulnerable, but she knew she was completely safe in her husband's embrace.

"My brother cannot stay," White Owl said. "He will eat and then head back to our village."

"I'll get the meal done quickly so you can be on your way," she said as she narrowed her gaze at Two Feathers. She saw a brief look of surprise filter through his expression as he realized that she was not intimidated by him any longer.

As she pulled away from White Owl to return to her cooking duties, he yanked her back to him and kissed her mouth hard. When he turned her loose, she could not help a wide grin. It was as if he wanted to prove to his brother how much desire he had for her.

White Owl retrieved her heavy wool coat from the cave. She had stuffed only a few articles of clothes and necessities in her bag when she had left her parents' house, and now she was grateful she had thought to pack this coat. It was easier for her to maneuver around the fire pit, and she busied herself with stirring the rabbit stew and getting ready for the meal. The men sat beside the fire and smoked from a long pipe.

The brothers spoke in Ute most of the time, but their conversation was interlaced with occasional words in the white man's language, and Rose could tell they were discussing different family members. She longed to ask how Sage and Shy Girl were doing, but decided to wait to ask White Owl about them after his brother left, which she hoped would be soon.

Once the stew was finished and ladled into wooden bowls to cool, Rose followed the Ute custom and placed the bowls in front of the men, then retreated to the other side of the fire to wait for them to eat before she served herself. When it had just been her and White Owl, they had eaten every meal together, but she didn't want to chance making Two Feathers resent her even more. She noticed that White Owl stared at her with a quizzical expression for a moment, and then he nodded and grinned. Rose was grateful that she had remembered this custom from her brief time in the Ute village.

After the men had finished eating Rose ate her meal and was pleasantly surprised at how good the stew tasted. She smiled to herself . . . she really was getting the hang of cooking over an open fire. White Owl and Two Feathers were standing by the horses, and it appeared that Two Feathers was getting ready to leave. He had not said another word to her after the fire incident. Now he held the reins to his horse in one hand. His other hand was waving through the air as if he was angry about something. But they were not shouting. Rose could barely hear their voices. She couldn't wait for him to leave so that she could ask White Owl why he had come. Whatever it was, she sensed that it wasn't to bring good news. Something was going on. She just hoped her husband would tell her everything once they were alone again.

Rose busied herself with cleaning up after the meal while the men continued their heated but hushed conversation. Then Two Feathers said something loudly in Ute and jumped up on his horse. Without a glance at her or back at his brother, he kicked his horse in the sides and galloped out of the camp. Until he disappeared from view in the deep canyon, White Owl remained rooted to the spot. He finally turned and began to walk back to Rose. He did not meet her inquiring stare as he reached the fire pit and stood beside her to warm his hands over the flames.

"Why did he really come today?" Rose asked.

White Owl stared into the fire but did not answer right away.

"Has something bad happened? Please tell me," Rose pleaded. A hard knot was forming in the pit of her stomach and making it feel as if her food was about to come back up.

"There has been a battle at the agency," he finally said in a flat voice.

"What?" Rose cried. "How bad was it?" She saw White Owl take a deep breath and sensed what his next words would be.

"The men there were all killed," he answered.

"A-all of them," Rose gasped. The smiling face of Frank Weber, the owner of the general store, flashed through her mind. And Nathan Meeker and all the other men she had seen around the agency when she had been there in the past. She swallowed the taste of bile in her mouth.

"What about the-the women and children?"

White Owl picked up a log and tossed it on the fire, even though it was not necessary. He shrugged. "They were all taken captive."

"Oh no!" Tears streamed down her face. The cold air made them feel like ice. She had heard enough stories about what happened to white women who were taken captive to know that the women from the agency were undoubtedly suffering unthinkable indignities, if they were even still alive. She wrapped her arms around herself and stared into the fire as she tried to wipe away the horrible images.

She had met all three of the women. There was the elderly wife of Nathan Meeker, the sweet, gentle Arvilla, and their adventurous daughter, Josephine, who was a couple of years older than Rose and loved by everyone who met her. Then there was the beautiful and quiet Mrs. Price. She was even younger than Rose, but she and her young husband already had two very small children. That poor girl was a widow now, Rose realized, but she could not even begin to comprehend what Mrs. Price and those two babies must be going through.

"I have to go home. I have to make sure my family is safe," Rose said in barely more than a whisper.

White Owl continued to stare into the flames. "Your family is safe. Two Feathers told me. The battle was nearly three weeks ago. There is no need to go back now."

"Three weeks?" Rose repeated. She couldn't imagine all that horror had happened three weeks ago and they were just hearing about it now. "I still have to go." Rose continued to stare into the fire as she added, "I have to go home today and see with my own eyes that my family is safe."

White Owl sighed deeply. "I will take you back. But I was hoping that your home was with me now."

Rose heard the sorrow in his voice as the meaning of his words pierced her heart. She turned to face him and encircled his waist with her arms. He pulled her against him, and she rested her head against his broad chest. "You are everything—everything—to me, my husband. I did not mean it the way I said it. It's just that they, my family—"

"I know," he interrupted. "And the time was coming for us to go back anyway. It would be foolish to stay here all winter."

She had hoped he would tell her once she saw her family, they could come back here and never leave again. But he was right—it was foolish to think they could live this idyllic life forever. Being in this magical place, it was even harder to imagine the horror of what must have happened at the White River Agency. But they couldn't hide away from the rest of the world forever, and knowing that all those men had been killed and thinking about what those women and babies must be going through, she could not imagine that everything would ever be the same again.

"I will pack," she said as a crushing sadness invaded her.

"There is something I must tell you first," White Owl added.

An added sense of dread gripped at Rose's heart. "What is it?" she asked tentatively.

"When we were still at my village, before we left to come here for the wedding trip, I knew."

Rose stared up at him and shrugged. "What—what did you know?"

"I knew the battle was going to happen soon, and that is why I was in such a hurry to get you away. I spoke to Chief Jack and my father about it before we left. They understood, and they both agreed we should stay here until it was over." His voice grew pleading as he added, "Please understand that I did it to protect you, only because I love you so much."

She pulled away from White Owl and took a step back as her mind tried to grasp what he had just told her. His rush to leave the village had seemed odd, but she had thought that he was as eager to start their married life together as she was. Now she learned his actions were also to protect her.

She looked up at him. His handsome face was a mask of sadness and worry; his raven gaze was tender and undeniably filled with the love he had just spoken of.

"I understand, too," she said sorrowfully. But she could not talk any more about it. She clutched at the hard knot in her chest and turned away as she headed for the cave. The wind nearly knocked her over as she climbed up the slope, but she gritted her teeth and pushed on. Once she reached the shelter of the cave, the reality of everything that he had just told her hit her even harder than the vicious wind blowing outside. She threw her hands over her face and let the loud sobs consume her. Her body shook as the fiery tears streamed down her face.

Even the feel of White Owl's arms embracing her when he joined her in the cave could not console her this time. She allowed him to turn her around, and she buried her face against his chest. For the first time since she had fallen in love with him, being in his arms did not make her feel safe, because she knew that once they left this secluded sanctuary, nothing would ever be the same again.

Outside the cave, the wind continued to wail, and now a hard, fast rain was pelting down on the ground. Under different circumstances, the storm would have seemed miraculous after the long drought. Now it only added to Rose's feeling of gloom.

White Owl cradled her in his arms as they sat beside the fire pit in the cave. She had long since cried herself into a numb stupor. She had resigned herself that there was no way they were going to be able to leave today. It would be impossible to travel in this kind of weather.

Sitting in her husband's lap, she felt like a helpless, confused child. As much as she needed to make sure her family had truly not been affected by the battle with the Utes, another part of her wished the weather would never clear up so that she would not have to face the harsh realities of what had happened. If there was one thing she was certain of, however, it was that there was no way now her family would ever accept her marriage to White Owl.

"I don't entirely blame the Utes for what happened at the agency," Rose whispered after a long, deafening silence. She guessed they had probably been sitting in the cave for a couple of hours or longer. "I know this trouble has been brewing for a very long time."

"Since the white men first came to our lands," White Owl replied quietly.

His words were spoken in a tone that made her choke up with tears again. It was beyond her comprehension how much his people must have suffered at the hands of the white men. But she still couldn't excuse the fact that some of his tribesmen had killed all those innocent men at the agency and taken the women and children captive.

It was such a twisted story of how one wrong created another wrong, and as White Owl had just reminded her, it had been going on since the beginning of time. She rested her head against her husband's firm chest. At least he had not participated in the battle. She would not allow herself to think about what a drastic difference that would have made to their lives.

It rained steadily for two days and nights. Vermillion Creek was almost full again, and new gullies had appeared everywhere where only little ditches had been previously. The mud that clung to the sandstone rocks and overtook the sparse vegetation in the meadow was like clay and made walking any distance nearly impossible, because it would stick to their boots and suck their feet down into its murky depths. It was not until the sun had shined for two full days that White Owl decided it was suitable to travel.

As Rose left the cave for the last time, she turned to look at the cozy alcove that had been their shelter, their love nest, and their first home as man and wife. She tried not to be sad . . . Someday, she knew they would come back here. Until then, she would remember every second that they had lived and loved in this hidden cave among the sandstone cliffs and sacred pictures of the people who had inhabited this special place before them. The magical memories they had created here would remain in their hearts forever.

Chapter Nineteen

The trip home seemed to go much faster than when they had traveled to Vermillion Basin more than two months ago. Rose thought this was backward, because she had been so eager to start their wedding trip, and now she was dreading the situation they would find when they got home.

White Owl had told her that his tribe usually traveled south for the winter months, so once she made sure her family was safe and dealt with their wrath, she knew they would be traveling again to the winter location. White Owl told her the winter camp was close to the home of Chief Ouray. Rose had heard stories and read articles in the newspapers about the great Ute chief and his wife, Chipeta, when she had still been living in Denver. They were both exceptionally educated in the ways of the whites and were great advocates of making peace between their people and the white men. She remembered reading that Chief Ouray was considered to be the "the White Man's Friend." How did he feel about the events that had transpired at the White River Agency? she wondered.

Lost in her worries about what they might encounter once they reached the Ute village, Rose finally became aware that White Owl was leading them through dense trees and avoiding as many open areas as possible. Her anxiety increased.

"White Owl," she called out as she pushed Molly forward to catch up to Niwaa. "Why are we going this way? Isn't there a shorter route to the village?"

He glanced around nervously before turning his attention to her. "There has recently been a battle in this area. Soldiers will be hunting for all Utes. We should not make too much noise."

Rose drew in an uneasy breath. "But it was Agent Meeker's fault. He wanted to plow up your racetrack." An unfamiliar sound made her jump, but it was nothing more than a chipmunk scurrying up a tree trunk. "Why would they be hunting for us? We weren't even here."

"They won't be hunting you. But it will not matter where I was. I am Ute, and that is all they will care about."

"What are you saying?" Rose demanded as she pushed Molly to keep up with Niwaa. "I will tell them that we were far away and—"

"You are not listening," White Owl cut in. He pulled on his reins and stopped Niwaa, and then reached out and grabbed Molly's reins to halt her, too. "You are white, so you don't know what it is like to be hunted down like you are a wild animal, to have your people slaughtered before your eyes, your home burned to the ground, and to live with the daily fear that eventually there will be nothing left to even prove that you ever existed." His tone had grown angry, and his jaw squared as he dropped Molly's reins. "Maybe your father is right." He kicked Niwaa in the sides, and the horse lunged forward.

His harsh words echoed through Rose's mind and made her stomach feel like a boulder had just settled in it. "White Owl, wait," she called as she sent Molly galloping to catch up with him. He did not stop, even as she rode up beside him again.

"What do you mean—my father is right?" she said. She held her breath as she waited for his reply.

He rode for a couple moments before he spoke again. "Our people are enemies, Wild Rose. We don't belong together." His voice sounded strained as he tried to appear unemotional.

Rose's eyes blurred and her head begin to pound. She pulled on Molly's reins and stopped as White Owl rode ahead. "No," she choked out. "You don't mean that." He kept riding, getting farther away. Rose couldn't breathe; she couldn't move; she couldn't go on living without him.

White Owl stopped Niwaa several hundred yards ahead. He sat straight in the saddle without turning around for what seemed like forever to Rose. The silent tears that fell from her blurry eyes left trails down her dusty cheeks and landed unnoticed on the bosom of her plaid shirt. When he dismounted and began to walk toward her, Rose was certain her heart was about to be ripped from her breast, and she would be left with nothing but a gaping hole in her chest. His dark features were set in an expression she had never seen on his face before, and she couldn't help wondering whether she was gazing upon him for the last time.

When he stopped beside her horse, he did not meet her teary gaze. He avoided her eyes as he reached up and pulled her from Molly's back, but before Rose had a chance to react he hugged her against him so tightly that she was sure he would break her ribs.

"I am sorry," he whispered into her ear. "I am so sorry," he repeated.

It took Rose a moment to realize what he was saying, because she had been so prepared for him to be saying good-bye. Her arms rose so that she could comb her fingers through his long hair; this was her reassurance that she wasn't dreaming.

"Forgive me," he added. He released his crushing hold on her and pulled back slightly so that he could look into her eyes. "What I said, it's true, but it doesn't matter. I can't live without you." White Owl's fingers pressed against her lips when she opened her mouth to speak.

"No, I was being foolish." His fingers moved from her mouth to her cheek. His trembling hand tenderly rested against the side of her face. "I am supposed to be a fierce warrior, but I am afraid, Wild Rose, so afraid of losing you, and it makes me say and do stupid things. I can't help but worry that your life will be miserable with me."

"It won't!" Rose cried. She felt the quivering in his hand and reached up to place her hand over his. "Never," she said firmly.

"When we return to the village, everything will be different. You have seen my people only when they are at peace, but now we are at war with your people. Some will be hostile toward you, and I will not tolerate that. And your father—"

Rose shook her head vigorously. She remembered Two Feathers' coldness and wondered if the rest of the family would feel the same way about her now. "No, you cannot fight with your own people because of me." She didn't respond to his mention of her father, because the thought was too terrifying.

White Owl sighed. "We can't let our families tear us apart."

"We won't," Rose said strongly. She rose on her toes and kissed his frowning mouth. He instantly returned her kiss. It did not seem possible to her that anyone could tear them apart, no matter how hard they might try. Their love was too strong. Nothing and no one could come between them.

"I will take you to your parents' home so that you can make sure they are safe," White Owl announced as they drew nearer to Milk Creek. The sun was hanging low in the western sky, and since the days were getting shorter with the approaching winter, it would be dark soon. "I will go to the village while you are there and come back to get you in the morning."

Rose felt a rush of panic. "No, I don't want to be away from you tonight. I'll come to the village with you and then to my parents' in the morning."

White Owl smiled. "I didn't want to sleep alone

tonight either." He tossed his long hair over his shoulder and motioned for her to follow him.

Rose let Molly fall in behind Niwaa without another comment. They could deal with her family tomorrow. Tonight they would face his family. But if they were together, she was sure they could handle anything.

The village had been moved farther south after the battle, so it was late at night when they finally reached their destination. A Ute scout who had been standing watch a couple of miles from the village directed them to the new location. Rose could feel the tension in the air the moment they dismounted from their horses.

Although it was a cold autumn night, there were only a few fires among the scattering of tepees, and the village was about a fourth of the size that it had been when Rose and White Owl had left for their wedding trip.

As they walked through the village, they were observed with quiet curiosity. A couple of the men called out a greeting to White Owl, but no one even looked in Rose's direction. The quiet, dark village had an eerie feel, and Rose was glad when they reached the tepee of White Owl's parents.

Strong Elk was sitting in front of a cold fire pit. A colorful woven blanket was wrapped around his shoulders. He looked up as the couple approached, and in the semidarkness Rose could see him grin.

"My oldest son has returned," he called as he jumped to his feet and tossed the blanket to the ground. He stepped forward and the two men embraced. "It is good to see you, my son," Strong Elk said as he backed away from his son. He looked at Rose and added, "Has my son treated you well?"

"Yes, he has," she answered. She stepped up and stood beside her husband as she once again marveled at the kindness and understanding of his family. She couldn't imagine her father and brothers would be so generous tomorrow. As this thought passed through her mind, Two Feathers walked up to the fire pit. His attitude had obviously not changed toward her. She could feel his hateful glare on her the instant he looked at her. She looped her arm through White Owl's for comfort.

"You are here at last. I thought you might have turned your back on your people altogether." Two Feathers' voice was filled with venom.

White Owl did not flinch at his brother's insinuation. "Good to see you, too," he retorted. He turned toward his father again. "We will stay here tonight and then go to Wild Rose's family in the morning."

"You must be careful. The leaders in Washington are threatening to make us leave our homelands. It is said that they will shoot any Ute who does not go to the reservation in Utah. They are very angry about the agency."

Rose felt White Owl stiffen beside her. He asked the question that was weighing heavily on her mind. "Where are the captives—the women and the children?"

"They were taken to Chief Ouray's house a few

days ago, but they have been returned to their own people now," Strong Elk replied. "They are all safe. Still, the chiefs in Washington want to punish all our people because of the killings at the agency and of Major Thornburg and his men at Milk Creek."

Rose's blood felt as though it had turned to ice in her veins. Milk Creek was much too close to her parents' ranch. She clutched White Owl's arm for support, and he placed his hand over hers.

"What happened at Milk Creek?" White Owl asked. His brother had forgotten to mention that incident when he had visited them at Vermillion Basin.

Strong Elk motioned for them to sit with him on the ground. "Two Feathers, make us a fire," he ordered.

Rose looked at the other warrior out of the side of her eye, trying to glimpse his reaction to being ordered around by his father. Much to her surprise, he did not argue and stalked to a pile of wood outside of the tepee and did as he was told. The expression on his face, however, was filled with fury.

"After the warriors killed Meeker and the others at the agency, soldiers came from the north," Strong Elk began once they were all seated on the ground. "We killed their leader, Major Thornburg, and many more soldiers at Milk Creek. The soldiers were stupid and didn't know how to fight. They tried to hide in the field where we could see them and pick them off one by one."

"You took part in the battles?" White Owl asked tentatively.

"I did not go to the agency—only the younger ones fought there. But I fought at Milk Creek beside my brothers."

When Strong Elk finally finished telling them the entire story, Rose felt as if she was going to pass out. Nine men had been killed in the carnage at the White River Agency, and all of the buildings had been burned to the ground. The women and children had been in captivity for twenty-three days before they had been released. Major Thornburg's battalion of soldiers, who had been coming from Wyoming to help alleviate the situation at the agency, had lost fourteen men, and numerous others had been wounded. Several warriors had been killed or injured. White Owl was right . . . everything was different now.

"My brother should have been here to fight," Two Feathers spat. His attention was focused directly on Rose.

She looked back at White Owl. His jaw was squared and his mouth clamped tightly shut as if he was trying to hold in his words. She was relieved to see that Strong Elk was glaring at his youngest son.

"We have talked of this, Two Feathers, and we will not talk of it again," the older warrior said sternly.

"Are you proud of a son who hides behind the skirts of our enemies?" The contempt in his voice was heavy, and the expression on his face in the flickering firelight conveyed his rage.

White Owl sprang to his feet and faced his brother. His hands fisted at his sides. "It was decided by all of us that I would protect Wild Rose by taking her away from here. Even Jack thought we should leave."

"You could have sent her back to the whites where she belongs and stood beside your brothers in war. She has turned you into a woman!"

Rose jumped to her feet as the two brothers charged each other. She screamed, but stepped back when they both went crashing to the ground, barely missing the fire pit. Strong Elk shouted something in Ute, and before she realized it, a crowd of villagers surrounded the two men rolling on the ground. She was pushed back and could no longer see what was happening until she fought her way back to the front of the spectators. She opened her mouth to cry out to White Owl, but the words stuck in her throat.

Two Feathers was lying on his back in the dirt, and White Owl was kneeling on top of him with one knee pinning him to the ground and his forearm pressed against his neck. In his hand, he held his hunting knife, which was now pressed against Two Feathers' chest. Her insides froze with dread. For the first time since they had met, her husband looked savage and murderous.

She rushed to White Owl's side. He did not look up at her until she cried out to him. "No, he's your brother! I won't let you kill your own brother because of me."

White Owl remained unmoving for a few

minutes and kept his death grip on Two Feathers. Rose glanced at Two Feathers and was shocked to see him looking up at her with a smirk on his face. She stumbled back a step as she tried to control her fear. For one crazy second, she almost wished White Owl would plunge that blade into his brother's heart.

Strong Elk had walked up to stand beside Rose. An expression of pain contorted his face, but when she noticed the look of terror on Sage's face as she entered the circle, Rose's own agony seemed unimportant. These were her sons, and Rose could not imagine the heartbreak she must be feeling at this moment.

"I'll leave, and you'll never see me again if you kill him, White Owl," Rose said. She hoped her voice sounded stern, but she knew it was more shaky than strong. Now she finally had his attention. His eyes closed for a second. He slowly raised his arm from his brother's neck, but he kept the knife against his chest for another moment. Strong Elk ran up to his sons and grabbed Two Feathers as White Owl drew the knife away. Rose exhaled hard. They had been back for only a short time, and already they had encountered exactly the type of trouble that White Owl had predicted.

White Owl slowly rose and turned to give Rose a questioning look.

She stepped up to him. "I saw your mother's face. I had to do something."

Without replying, White Owl turned and walked away.

Rose watched him disappear into the darkness. She didn't understand what had just happened. They had promised only earlier today that they wouldn't allow their families to tear them apart. Was that promise about to be broken?

"Thank you," a soft voice said.

Rose turned to look at Sage. She shrugged, but could not speak because of the hard lump in her throat.

"He is angry, but he return to you," the older woman said softly.

"I know," Rose whispered. She attempted to smile at Sage, but couldn't pull it off.

The older woman put her arm around Rose's shoulder. "Come rest now. I have made a bed for you and my son in our tepee for tonight. In morning we put up your tepee."

Rose nodded and let Sage guide her into the tepee. A small fire in the center of the tepee created a cozy atmosphere and made Rose think of the cave they had lived in for the past couple of months. How she wished they were still there now. She was surprised that Cloud Woman and Shy Girl were not there, but she was too distraught about White Owl to ask about them.

She gratefully sank down to the thick mattress Sage had made of blankets. The long trip had taken its toll on her body, and the fight between White Owl and Two Feathers had drained her mind of all coherent thoughts. Still, she was certain that she would not be able to sleep without White Owl beside her. Within minutes of lying down, though, she was asleep.

Her slumber was disturbed with fleeting nightmares of the men at the agency being slaughtered and crying babies and flashes of dead soldiers. She awoke drenched in sweat and feeling disoriented until she became aware of where she was. When she realized that White Owl was lying beside her, the nightmares dissipated into relief.

She took a deep breath and wiped her hand across her sweating brow. He was lying on his side with his back to her. She reached out to touch him, but then pulled her hand back. Her heart ached for the pain her husband must feel, and even more because she knew there was no way she could help him.

"I'm awake," he whispered.

Rose exhaled the breath she had been holding as he rolled over onto his back. She immediately snuggled up against him. His arm cradled her securely at his side.

"I'm so sorry, White Owl. I never wanted to cause you and your fam—"

"You did not cause this," he cut in. "It has been brewing since we were little."

"But I—" Her words were cut off once again when he put his hand up to her mouth.

"I will not allow you to blame yourself." He sighed heavily. "Your brothers and father will feel the same."

The blood in Rose's veins turned ice cold. Her father and Tate would be even worse than Two Feathers. "I must go see them alone."

White Owl was silent for a moment. He exhaled sharply. "I will ride with you, but you are right. You should talk to your family alone first and try to make them understand our love. If I am there, they will only be concerned with putting a bullet between my eyes."

Rose blinked several times to wipe that horrible image from her mind. As for making them understand? That was not going to happen. Still, she had to go back and see them one last time, especially her mother and Donavan. Then she could move on with her life and the peaceful future she envisioned with her handsome husband, in spite of the sense of impending doom that settled heavily in her heart at this moment.

Chapter Twenty

Although everything at White Owl's village had changed, nothing at the Adair ranch looked any different. Rose glanced back over her shoulder at White Owl. He waited farther back on the ridge so that he was out of sight. He gave her an encouraging smile. Rose forced herself to smile back.

He looked so regal sitting on his big black stallion. Wearing a complete buckskin suit he looked more handsome than usual. She had braided the front sections of his hair and the long braids hung over his chest. The remainder of his luscious locks that she loved to run her fingers through hung down his back. A beaded headband encircled his head. The only things that detracted from his beautiful image were the thick belts of ammunition he wore around his narrow waist and angled across his broad chest. A rifle hung from his saddle, reminding Rose of the grave danger they faced in this area now.

She blew him a kiss. His smiled widened, and he nodded his head. When he waved back and turned to ride away, Rose had to wipe away a tear. It was good that he had been strong enough to ride away, because she knew she wouldn't have been able to be the first one to leave. Even now, it took all of her restraint to keep from kicking Molly in the sides and galloping after him. But she had to be as strong as he was being and take care of unfinished business.

Besides, he would be back to get her in the morning.

Rose hunched up her shoulders as a frosty blast of wind whipped around her. The weather was turning colder, and dark clouds were gathering overhead. She would spend the night apart from White Owl for the first time since she had left here over two months ago. It was going to be a long, cold night.

She drew a deep breath and turned back toward her family homestead. With a gentle nudge, she led Molly down the hill. Before she had even ridden all the way down the slope, Donavan spotted her. He had been getting water from the well, but he had dropped the full bucket on the ground when he saw her.

"Ma! Pa! Rose is back," he yelled as he ran toward her. "Rose! Rose!" he cried over and over as they drew nearer to one another.

The tears flooding down her face were uncontrollable now, and when she was still several hundred yards away from him, Rose jumped down from Molly's back and ran the rest of the way until her little brother was wrapped in her embrace. Although it had not been that long since she had seen him, it seemed as if he had grown several inches taller, or maybe it had been such a long time since they had actually hugged that she had forgotten how fast he was growing into a young man. He was now taller than she was, and she was certain he hadn't been when she left two months earlier.

When they finally pulled apart, Rose's gaze was drawn to the small woman who was standing a couple of feet away.

"Mama," she gasped through her tears. She held her arms open and waited as her mother stepped forward hesitantly as if she was afraid of her. Taking the initiative, Rose stepped forward and threw her arms around her mother. "I'm sorry I left the way I did," she cried as her mother tightened her hold around her.

As her mother cried and they hugged, she looked over her mother's head and glimpsed her father and Tate. They had stopped a good distance back. Each held a rifle and their expressions were identical, filled with hate and disgust.

"Are you here to stay?" Colleen whispered in Rose's ear.

Rose choked back her tears as she realized the fearful tone in her mother's voice. "No, Mother, I am not," she replied. She pulled back from her mother and met the other woman's sorrowful gaze. "I am only here to apologize for leaving the way I did. And to make sure that you are all safe after what happened at the agency. Then I will be returning to my husband." She said the words as loudly as her shaking voice would allow. Beside her,

Donavan moaned. Her mother's face drained of all color.

"So it's true then," her mother said. "What you wrote in your note?"

Rose reached out and clasped her mother's hand; it lay limply in her own. "Please try to understand. I love him more than my own life."

"Well, that's good, 'cause your life is worthless if you are still with that Injun," Tate spat as he walked closer. Her father had not moved.

Rose dropped her mother's hand and stepped away from all of them. "Please hear me out," she pleaded loud enough for her father to hear. He took several steps closer. "Father, I am begging you to listen to me." She took a couple shaky steps toward him.

His face was red, and the fury in his blue eyes made them look as hard as ice; his lips were drawn together so tightly that they barely formed a thin white line above his chin. Inwardly, she cringed. "I will have my say and then I will leave, and you will not have to look at me again."

"Paddy, please?" Colleen cried out. "She's our daughter."

"And a filthy squaw," Tate growled between gritted teeth. He raised his rifle.

Colleen screamed, and Donavan ran to place himself between his older brother and sister. Rose could not move in her dazed state. Did her own twin hate her enough to kill her? The events of the previous night flashed through her mind . . .

White Owl and Two Feathers, wrestling on the ground and then the knife pressed against Two Feathers' heart. She swallowed hard. How could two people falling in love cause so much animosity?

"Tate!" Paddy yelled. He walked up to the group and faced his eldest son. "I know how you feel, but this ain't gonna solve the problem."

Tate stared at his father for an instant and then slowly lowered the gun. His head dropped. Paddy reached out and easily took the rifle from his hand. Then, turning back to the rest of his family, he said flatly, "You came back for a reason, and we will hear you out."

"T-th—" Rose's voice would not work. She felt her mother's arm around her shoulder and Donavan's hand clasp ahold of hers.

"We'll set at the table and talk like a rational family," Colleen said.

"I don't want her in the house," Tate announced.

"Enough, boy." Paddy glanced at Rose with narrowed eyes. "You say what you came to say." He shook his head and added, "And you're welcome in the house." He cast a warning glance at Tate, whose face was now redder than his father's.

Rose was led forward by her mother and younger brother, but she felt like her legs were made of lead. Although she had known what to expect from Tate and her father, actually hearing how much they hated her was worse than she had ever imagined.

The delicious odor of freshly baked cornbread filled the air, and the interior of the sprawling ranch house was warm and comforting, especially compared to the dropping temperature outside. But Rose no longer felt welcome there. She pictured the cozy cave at Vermillion Basin and fought back tears. She sat down at the table and stared blankly at her father as he sat across from her. They were the only two to sit down.

Her mother rushed to pour her a cup of coffee and placed the mug and a large chunk of cornbread in front of her. Rose didn't even look at the food or drink because she knew nothing would be able to pass over the strangling lump in her throat.

"Speak," her father ordered after a couple of minutes of uneasy silence.

Rose jumped at the sound of his impatient command. "S-so you found my note?"

"That you were running off with some Ute buck and not to try to find you." He slammed his fist down on the tabletop. "Do you have any idea what that did to your ma?"

Rose flinched but tried to stay calm. She glanced at her mother. "I know, and I am sorry. I just knew that you—none of you—would understand if I tried to tell you how I feel about White Owl."

A hateful chortle came from Tate. "White Owl," he repeated like he had tasted something repulsive. He opened his mouth to say more, but Paddy's look of warning silenced him.

"I-I—" Paddy's face reddened again, and he had to take a moment before he could speak again. "I guess that was what you were doin' on all those long rides—meetin' up with that—that—" His mouth clamped shut as if he couldn't even say the words out loud.

Rose stared down at the full mug of coffee sitting before her. "Yes," she mumbled. Her lies had come back to haunt her. She should have just told them right from the start about meeting White Owl, but her fear had prevented it, and now she was realizing how much worse she had made the entire situation. She heard a disgusted grunt from Tate's direction.

"You've been with him all this time?" Tate's hate-filled voice rang out in more of an accusation than a question.

Rose slowly nodded and looked back up at her father. "He's my husband and I love him with—"

Her words were cut off sharply when her father's anger overwhelmed him. The heavy wooden table went rolling over when he grabbed the edge and sent it flying onto its side. Rose felt the burn of the hot coffee when the overturned mug fell in her lap. She cried out and jumped up, knocking the chair over and then tripping over the chair and crashing backward on the hard wood planks of the floor.

Her mother was kneeling beside her. "Rosaline, are you all right?" Her hand was on Rose's forehead as if she was trying to take her temperature.

Rose stared up at her mother as her image danced like waves before her eyes. As her vision began to clear, she was aware of pain in her back where she landed on the floor and the burn of the coffee on her thigh, but neither injury induced as much pain as her father's rage. She blinked and slowly nodded her head. "I'm fine," she said quietly. Her mother helped her sit up, but it took a second for her head to stop spinning so that she could stand up on her quivering legs.

"Paddy!" Colleen screamed. "Why?"

Paddy Adair was standing on the other side of the overturned table. "Get your clothes changed, Rosaline. I'm takin' you to Denver now!"

His words spun through Rose's foggy mind. "No—you can't make me go," she retorted in as forceful a voice as she could speak. "I won't . . . I'm a married woman!"

"You're my daughter, and that . . . that so-called marriage ain't legal." He looked at his wife. "Go with her and get her a bag of clothes. Don't think I won't hunt her down this time if you let her leave." His tone was so filled with venom that Rose felt her mother shiver.

Rose stumbled blindly into her old room as her mother pulled her along with her. Once they were on the other side of the heavy curtain that separated the room from the rest of the house, her shock finally began to fade into disbelief and then refusal. "He can't make me go," she stated as her mother began rushing around the room grabbing clothes and stuffing them into a cotton satchel.

"Please, Rose, don't argue with him. I've never seen him so angry." Her mother's panic was apparent. "I am afraid for you, so please don't fight with him anymore."

Rose started to walk over to her mother and realized that her leg and back were filled with shooting pains from her hard fall. She limped over to where Colleen was shoving toiletries into the bag with visibly shaking hands. She reached out and grabbed her mother's arm. "I am married, Mother, to a man I love so much that I would rather die than live without him."

Colleen ceased all movements and looked over at her daughter. Their blue gazes locked. Rose could see the sorrow in her mother's eyes, as well as her own reflection shimmering back at her. Her mother was her only hope now.

"You have to go to Denver," Colleen said in a hoarse whisper.

Rose's arms dropped against her sides with a thud as her mother's unexpected demand echoed through her mind. No! No! No! she wanted to scream, but she knew it would not matter. She could see the terror in her mother's eyes and realized for the first time just how frightened her mother was of her father.

Rose closed her eyes and turned away as the hot tears once again rolled from her eyes. Without turning to face her mother again, she said quietly, "He will be coming here to get me in the morning. Can you at least tell him where I am? Please, can you do that one last thing for me, Mother?"

A sharp pain sliced through Rose's breast as she waited for her mother's reply. "Rosaline, once you reach Denver you will realize what a mistake these past few months have been, and you will be able to move on with your life. No one will ever have to know."

Rose threw her hand over her heart. This time it truly felt like it had just been torn out of her chest, and there was nothing more than a hollow hole left. He would come here tomorrow and she would be gone. No one was going to tell him where she was, and that was more than she could bear.

As the room suddenly began to spin before her eyes, and then went completely black, Rose felt herself slipping down to the floor once again. The darkness was welcoming—safe. In her dreams she was in White Owl's arms again.

Chapter Twenty-one

The blizzard lasted for three days. It had started late in the afternoon on the day that White Owl had left Wild Rose at her family's ranch. He had tried to head back to the ranch that same evening, but his father had told him to wait to see if the weather cleared by morning. She wasn't expecting him until then, anyway.

The next day was a complete whiteout, and traveling was impossible with the blinding snow falling sideways in the freezing wind that howled across the land. The villagers began to pack up their belongings so that at the first break in the weather, they could begin to move farther south. The long hot autumn and drought of the past summer had rapidly turned into a vicious winter, and already some of the tribe had headed to warmer grounds. Strong Elk's second wife, Cloud Woman, and his young daughter, Shy Girl, had left a few days earlier with the first group to begin setting up the winter camp.

White Owl was crazy without his woman for this long. One night apart had seemed like an eternity, but three nights was pure torture. His only consolation was that she was safe with her family, and once he went to get her, they would never be apart again. It was a good thing, he tried to convince himself, that she was staying with them this long. He had no doubt that they had been furious at first, but perhaps the longer they had been forced to be under the same roof during the storm, they had been able to overcome some of the anger.

He wanted his Wild Rose to be content when they continued on their life's journey, and he knew that she was deeply troubled by the way she had left her parents' home before. White Owl had convinced himself this storm had probably been beneficial, even if it meant he had to spend three endless nights alone under the fur robes of the tepee he had erected in anticipation of her return.

He glanced around the tepee as he put his heavy bear-fur coat on over his buckskin suit. He would be making love to his Wild Rose in here tonight. But by tomorrow, if the weather stayed decent, they would probably be taking the tepee down again so that they could begin the winter trek south. The thought of the long cold winter ahead did not seem so harsh now that he had his beautiful flame-haired wife to keep him warm.

The trip across Milk Creek and to the Adair property took longer than White Owl planned because of the heavy wet snow and the cold, relentless wind that still blew against him and Niwaa. With the slow progress they were making, it was late afternoon by the time he reached the ridge above the ranch. He was more than a little anxious to get his wife back, which was why he was not using his usual caution as he started down the slope. When the shot rang out and whizzed just inches away from his arm, it took him a second to even realize what was happening. Niwaa, however, was aware of the danger immediately, and while his master had hesitated to react, the horse twirled around and began charging back up the hill.

When White Owl's shock began to fade, he pushed Niwaa to the top faster as another bullet dug into the snow just a few feet beside them. At the top of the ridge, he jumped from Niwaa's back and pulled the rifle from his saddle as he dove face-first down on the ground. Since he had not been paying attention, he was not even sure where the shots were being fired from or whether or not there was only one shooter. He scooted on his stomach through the snow along the ledge until he found a protruding rock to hide behind. He slowly raised his head above the rock and surveyed the ranch. There was nothing to give him a clue as to where the attack was coming from.

Long minutes passed, and White Owl couldn't stand the wait. He clasped his rifle tightly in his hand and raised up slightly as he yelled as loud as possible. "I do not want to fight. I only come for my wife." He ducked back down behind the rock in case the reply was a bullet. Another long pause followed, and finally, a response.

"She's gone. She doesn't want to see you again."
White Owl hunkered down behind the rock

and tried to absorb the man's words. They didn't register in his mind. He rose up again.

"Where is my wife?" he demanded.

"I told you. She's gone. She left the minute you finally brought her home. She doesn't want to see you again," was the immediate reply.

White Owl fell back down on his knees. The man's words raced through his head. He felt like he had just been punched in the gut. No, it was not possible. He leaned forward and raised up again. "I don't believe you."

There was a pause before the man answered. "If you put down your weapon, I'll prove it to you."

The punch in his belly felt more like someone was shoving a long spear into him now. He fell back on his heels again. The love they had shared in the past few months flashed through his mind in vivid detail. There was no way that he could believe that she had left him voluntarily. She loved him as much as he loved her, or so he had thought. He swallowed the metal taste in his mouth and felt a sick feeling wash through his body.

"I'm putting my gun down and coming out," he hollered. As he rose to his feet, he raised his hands in the air to show the shooter that he no longer held his weapon. He took a step to the side, exposing himself completely. Waiting the next couple of seconds felt like a lifetime.

At last, a man stepped out from behind one of the small sheds. White Owl was surprised to see Rose's twin brother holding the gun. He had been prepared to meet her father first. He glanced around, expecting to see the older man step out from one of the other buildings, but only Tate walked forward.

"Take off that coat." Tate waved the rifle in a threatening manner. White Owl obliged and tossed the fur coat at his feet.

"Drop that knife on the ground," Tate ordered next. "And then come down very slowly."

White Owl did as instructed. He pulled the knife from its fringed sheath and let it fall to the ground. He began moving cautiously down the slope. He kept his hands raised the entire way. When he was within several yards from the man, he stopped and waited for further instructions. The younger man was watching him through narrowed eyes with the rifle leveled at his chest. White Owl was still expecting the appearance of the old man, but so far, only Rose's twin had greeted him.

A movement at the house caught White Owl's attention and he glanced in that direction. He saw an older version of Rose, but with pale brown hair, and the younger brother, Donavan, standing on the stoop. Pepper, the troublesome black dog, came running toward him wagging his tail. He didn't bark or growl even once now.

"Tate," the woman called. "What are you doing? Are you crazy?"

"He doesn't believe that Rose left. I'm gonna prove to him that she doesn't want to be with him, and then he is gonna leave and never come back," Tate hollered. "Isn't that right?" he added as he motioned toward White Owl with his gun.

White Owl nodded slowly. The pain in his belly was radiating through his entire body. How could they prove something to him that couldn't possibly be true?

Tate shoved his rifle in White Owl's back and pushed him forward. As they approached the house, Rose's mother and little brother backed through the front door. By the time they had entered, the woman was standing across the room with a shotgun in her hands. The younger brother was beside his mother. White Owl looked around the room as his anxiety increased. Wild Rose was nowhere to be seen.

"What have you done to her?" he demanded from Tate in an angry tone.

Tate chortled in a hateful tone. "You talk pretty good for a savage. I told you, she left because she didn't want to see you again. She asked our pa to take her to the train in Rawlins on the very day you brought her back. She's headed back to Ireland right now where she'll be safe from the likes of you."

White Owl clenched his fists at his sides and fought to control his raging emotions. "I don't believe you. She would not leave me," he said as he clenched his jaw. He glanced at the woman and saw a strange expression flit across her face. Had he only imagined that she looked sad and regretful for one brief second?

"Well then, I said I can prove it," Tate retorted as he motioned with his head toward a doorway that was covered by a heavy woolen curtain. He shoved the gun in White Owl's side and pushed him toward the doorway.

White Owl moved forward as a feeling of dread overcame him. He could not imagine what was on the other side of the curtain, and he didn't want to know. But he had no choice. He pulled aside the thick curtain and stepped into the room.

"This was her room," Tate said. "Look around. She packed all her belongings and asked our father to take her as far away from here as possible."

As Tate's words penetrated his mind, White Owl turned back to the room. It was a room . . . just a room, void of anything personal that could distinguish it as Wild Rose's room. He stepped inside and took a closer look around. It wasn't until he noticed the shiny object lying on the bureau that he realized it was true.

There in the center of a delicate white lace doily was the shimmering gold heart necklace that he had seen her wear on so many occasions when they had met in the barn or she had come to watch him at the racetrack. His insides twisted into a tight ball, and his knees felt weak as the reality settled in to his aching heart. She was gone.

"See, I told you, Injun," Tate spat out as White Owl remained unmoving in the middle of the room. "Now, I want you off of our land. I should just shoot you, but I will give you this one chance to leave. I will kill you if you ever come back."

White Owl stood mute. He couldn't speak, but he thought about provoking the younger man so that he would fulfill his threat to shoot him. Why would he want to take another breath if Wild Rose was not here anymore?

In a stupor, he stumbled out of the room and past Wild Rose's mother and younger brother. He let Tate use the gun to shove him out the front door and to the base of the slope that led away from the ranch. The stupid dog ran beside him, wagging his tail and jumping up against his leg as if he was his best friend. White Owl walked, but he couldn't talk, couldn't think, couldn't imagine a future without Wild Rose. Tate's ongoing threats went unheard as he trudged back up the slope and gathered up his things. He pulled himself up on Niwaa's back. His body felt as heavy as his heart. She was really gone. Only three days ago they had been planning a lifetime together. And now, she was headed to some faraway place called Ireland.

Colleen Adair stood outside the house with her shawl wrapped tightly around her shoulders. The wind was chilling, but her heart felt like a block of ice. She had helped destroy two lives in just a few days. It had nearly killed her to see the light gone from her daughter's blue gaze as she had left for Denver. After Rose had fainted and then been revived, she had been a changed girl. She had done exactly as they had told her—took a drink of water, ate a piece of cornbread, loaded up into the wagon beside her father, and left for Denver without saying another word. Her blank, lifeless eyes had stared straight forward the entire time, and as Colleen had watched the wagon pulling out of the yard, she felt so horrible she could barely live with herself.

When the storm had hit with such ferocity later that day, she had prayed that her husband would change his mind and come back. But the storm had continued to rage, and her regret had turned to resignation . . . and then White Owl had come.

When she saw the look in his dark eyes, she realized the extent of the horrible mistake they had made. It was more than apparent that White Owl loved her daughter more than she had ever imagined that a man could love a woman, and Rose loved him equally.

She watched as White Owl disappeared from view at the top of the ridge. Her hands clasped together as she prayed for forgiveness for her part in this terrible tragedy.

On his way back to the village, White Owl visited every place that he had ever been with his Wild Rose. The places along Milk Creek where they had first fallen in love and made love for the first time; he stopped under every tree where he had kissed her, and he even chanced going close to the agency so that he could see the spot where they had first met. He saw soldiers patrolling not far from the area where the racetrack was located, however, so he had not gone any farther. Several times he had found himself turning Niwaa around with the intention of riding back to the Adair ranch. He would make them tell him exactly where she was, and then he would go all the way to this place called Ireland and make her tell him to his face that she didn't want to be with him anymore.

But he knew that was foolish. Her family would never tell him anything more than they already had; they hated him and would do whatever it took to keep them apart. And besides, if it were true, if she really didn't want to be his wife anymore, he was sure he could not survive having her tell him this in person, anyway.

It was late when he returned to the village. He was grateful that nearly everyone was already asleep, because he was certain he could not have talked to anyone about the events of the day. He entered the cold, dark tepee—the same tepee he had planned to fill with her presence tonight. Instead, the blackness was filled with her ghost, because now she was the same as dead to him. If she really was in this faraway land called Ireland, he would never see her again. He stumbled through the darkness until his foot found the furs and blankets he had spread out for their bed, but he could not make himself lie down on them. Surrounded by only emptiness, he realized he could not be here at all. It would be too painful to be here without her.

He reached down and gathered up a couple of the

blankets and then made his way over to the area
where he had left his pack with his clothes and
other necessities. He grabbed the bag and headed
back out of the tepee. As he passed by his parents'
tepee, he hesitated. He knew he should tell them
that he was leaving, but they wouldn't understand.
With all the turmoil surrounding the tribe right
now because of the massacre at the agency, he knew
that they would want him to stay, at least until they
had moved to the winter location.

But he couldn't stay. There was only one place
he could be right now. He made his way back to
the horses, placed the saddle on Niwaa's back, and
led him away from the corral. Through the night
he rode until he reached the place where he had
camped with Rose on the first night of their wedding trip.

For the next two days, he rode and stopped in
the same areas they had stayed, until he was back
in Vermillion Basin.

As he rode down the mystical canyon with the
sacred etched pictures on the high cliffs, he felt a
strange transformation taking place inside him.
The past couple of days he had felt as if he was in
a daze. It didn't seem real that Wild Rose was really gone and that he was traveling back here without her.

But still he rode on as if he had no place else to
go. And now that he was here, he understood this
odd quest. The daze lifted as he rode out into the
meadow and glanced up where the hidden cave
was carved deep into the stone.

If he could no longer be with his Wild Rose, he could at least be where her memory would always remain. This was all he had left of her, and so this was where he would stay.

Chapter Twenty-two

Maggie Carroll was Colleen Adair's youngest sister, but she was nothing like Colleen. Although they had both been raised with a strict Irish upbringing, once they had immigrated to America, Maggie had fully embraced the more modern ways of their new country. She had turned down every suitor when they had asked for her hand in marriage because she claimed she had no desire to cater to a man and a passel of children—her own, anyway. It didn't bother her in the least bit that she was considered an old maid at the ripe old age of twenty-five. To her family's despair, she had chosen to be a teacher, which was the typical profession for spinsters.

Rose absolutely worshiped her Aunt Maggie. She was the most vibrant woman Rose had ever known, and she was also quite beautiful with her strawberry-blonde hair and flashing blue eyes. In some ways Rose looked even more like her aunt than she did her own mother, and people always mistook them for sisters, rather than aunt and niece.

When Rose and her father had arrived in Denver a few weeks earlier, Maggie had welcomed them with open arms, and much to Rose's relief she had not asked any questions until after Paddy Adair had left. Even then, she had only asked Rose if she was going to be all right. Still sick with heartbreak, Rose had not been able to tell her aunt why her father had deposited her on her doorstep without any advance warning. For those first few days after her father had left her, she had barely been able to talk at all. Every time she had even opened her mouth to speak, the tears that always teetered on the rims of her eyes would start to fall, and her voice would crack; it wasn't worth the effort to talk.

The worst part of this horror was wondering what had happened when White Owl had came to pick her up from her parents' ranch. They had planned to meet on the ridge at midmorning, but what had he done when she didn't show up? She prayed that he had gone down to the house and that her mother or Donavan had told him what happened to her and that Tate had not tried to shoot him. She would not consider that possibility. She spent the majority of the first leg of the journey sitting next to her father on the wagon seat and looking over her shoulder, hoping and praying that her husband would catch up with them before they reached Rawlins.

But the weather had turned bad, and she had no way of knowing whether the storm had also hit the Milk Creek area. Once they actually reached the city of Denver, she had given up on the dream that White Owl would catch up to them. Although she had no doubt that he would never believe she had left of her own free will, she still figured it would be up to her to get back to him now.

Denver was rapidly becoming a big city, and she could not imagine that he could find her here, even though he had been here in his youth. Plus, coming here would be far too dangerous for him after the White River Agency Massacre. Since her arrival, there was rarely a day that Rose didn't read something about the battle in the local paper. If the Colorado leaders—and most of the residents—had their way, the Utes would be completely exterminated, or at least, run out of the state altogether. The most recent headline in the newspaper had screamed, THE UTES MUST GO!

Rose's worries about her husband and his family were heavy crosses to bear, and she preferred to carry the burden alone. Thankfully, her Aunt Maggie never pried.

She asked Rose to help her grade her students' papers in the evenings, and she gave Rose chores to do during the day to help out around the little house that she lived in next to the schoolhouse along the Platte River, but she never asked any questions.

When Rose finally felt strong enough to leave the house and be around other people without wanting to cry, she agreed to go with Maggie to her grandparents' home for Thanksgiving. They lived in downtown Denver, where they owned a house and a general store. Rose had not even allowed Maggie to tell them that she was here yet, but since it was a holiday, Rose knew she could not disappoint her aunt. She had to go.

They planned to stay with her grandparents for four days, and there was no way her Grandmother Carroll was not going to drill Rose over and over again as to why she had returned to Denver unannounced.

As they sat down for breakfast before they left on Thanksgiving morning, Rose sighed and turned to look at her aunt. "Aunt Maggie, I need to talk to you."

"Of course, dear," Maggie said in a cheery voice as she sat at the little kitchen table opposite from Rose. "Are you feeling all right? You are awfully pale. You know, I heard that there was an illness going—"

"I'm fine," Rose cut in. "I just need to . . . to tell you why my father brought me here."

Maggie placed her napkin daintily in her lap. "Only if you are ready to talk about it." She smiled as she met Rose's gaze.

For the first time since she had arrived, Rose did not look away. She had to talk about it . . . and she especially needed to talk about him. "I was married, against my family's wishes." Rose did not let Maggie's gasp from her gaping mouth stop her. "Aunt Maggie, I was happier with him than I'd ever been. I had no idea it was possible to love someone so much—or be loved back so much."

Maggie's shocked look had now turned to one of confusion. "I don't understand. It's apparent how much you loved this man—your husband. I can't imagine why my sister wouldn't want you to be happy. She was much younger than you are now when she married Paddy." She clenched her teeth and added, "It was your father, wasn't it? I have always thought he was too domineering and your mother just lets him—"

"My husband is a Ute warrior," Rose interrupted again.

Maggie's tirade abruptly ended. "A-a what?" she finally asked.

Rose forced herself not to give in to the rising panic. She realized her aunt might hate the Utes as much as her father, but it was a chance she had to take.

"His name is White Owl, and he is the strongest, proudest, most loving man. When spring comes, I will go back to him. I would have already left, but his tribe moves to a warmer climate for the winter, and I'm afraid that I wouldn't be able to find them. And traveling this time of year would be foolish." Rose fidgeted in her chair. "I will completely understand if you want me to leave now, though."

Maggie stared at Rose with a shocked, glazed look upon her face. Her silence only served to increase Rose's anxiety.

Maggie finally took a deep breath and pressed her napkin to her forehead for a moment before speaking. "Well, I think it is wise not to travel at this time of year, dear." She put the napkin back in her lap, picked up her spoon, and began to stir her tea in the delicate flowered teacup that sat in front of her on the table. "And you know you are always welcome to stay here with me, so no more of that kind of talk."

She looked up from the teacup. "Thank you for confiding in me—finally. I cannot begin to understand what you have been through, but even I—the old maid schoolmarm—can understand about love. And it is more than obvious how much you must love this—this White Owl."

Rose forced back the tears that once again waited to be released from her eyes. She reached across the table and clasped Maggie's hand when she put the spoon down. "Thank you. But there's more."

Maggie chuckled and rolled her eyes upward. "More? What more could there possibly be, dear?"

Rose tightened the grip on her aunt's hand and exhaled sharply. "I'm—I'm . . . well, I think—no, I know—that I'm carrying his child." She felt Maggie's hand go limp as her face went ghastly white.

"Would you like me to leave now?" Rose said quietly as she turned loose of her aunt and pulled her own hand back down into her lap. "I probably should just go," she added when Maggie still made no comment or movement. Rose stood and turned. She needed to get away before the pain in her breaking heart rendered her unable to go.

"Wait," Maggie shouted. She rose to her feet and came to stand in front of Rose. "I was just thinking of what we will tell your grandparents."

"What?" Rose stuttered in confusion.

"Well, you know, they are old and a bit old-fashioned, too. I fear that they won't understand all this, and there is no need to make them fret over all the details. We will simply tell them that you married a cowboy or a soldier and he is off, um . . . Let's see, he's a soldier and he's off killing Indi—No, not that one . . . He's a soldier and he has been sent back East—"

"No soldiers," Rose said firmly. Soldiers and Indians were not a good mix.

"Oh, right," Maggie continued as if she hadn't been interrupted. "He's a cowboy then, from Wyoming, and he's off on a long cattle drive. Oh, how exciting—well, not as exciting as the actual truth, obviously. And you came here to wait out the winter until he returns."

Rose exhaled and shook her head. Her aunt was unbelievable. With barely more than a blink of her eyes—literally—Maggie had accepted Rose's story of how her family had thought she disgraced them, seemed completely unaffected that Rose was having her Ute husband's child, and was already planning a tall tale to protect her from everyone else's disapproval. There were not even words that she could find that would tell her aunt how much she loved and appreciated her. She threw her arms around her aunt's neck and squeezed until she heard Maggie laughing and trying to pry her arms away.

"Sorry, I just can't believe you. How is it possible that you and my mother are sisters?"

Maggie's expression grew more serious. "Your mother used to be a real Irish spitfire, but your father broke her spirit. Now, no more talk about sad things—we have a baby to plan for. When do you think—I mean—" Her face scrunched up, and she shrugged her shoulders as she pointed at Rose's stomach.

"Oh, in late spring, I am guessing. It could have happened anytime during—"

"Late spring it is," Maggie cut in, obviously not wanting to hear the details of the pregnancy. "We have plenty of time during the cold months to make baby clothes and get ready. Oh, how exciting!"

Her enthusiasm began to rub off on Rose, and for the first time since her father had made her leave the homestead and White Owl, she felt as though things might actually work out. She had no doubt that she would go back to Milk Creek to be with her husband again; only now she would be returning with his child, too. Her hands protectively covered the barely rounded area of her abdomen where he had planted the seed of their love.

Knowing that she still carried a part of him brought her joy, but her happiness could never be complete until she was with him again. It broke her heart to think that he wouldn't know about their baby until after it was born. She could vividly imagine the expression of happiness that would have lighted up his handsome face when she told him that she was carrying his child. She would never forgive her father for depriving them of this time together.

The winter days passed uneventfully. Christmas came and went. Rose and Maggie had their story perfected. A guilty pang shot through Rose whenever her dear grandmother and grandfather talked about their excitement to meet her cattle-driving cowboy husband in the spring and the thrill of being great-grandparents for the first time. Rose was not proud of lying to them, but the alternative was not an option.

Shortly after the New Year of 1880, Rose felt the baby move for the first time. She cried for hours because White Owl was missing all of these little firsts. But when she returned to his village in the spring, she would spend the rest of her life making sure he never missed anything again.

Chapter Twenty-three

The winter had started out harsh, but spring set in early. It was only early April, and already the Vermillion Basin was alive with new life. Snow melting from the towering mountain peaks sent flowing waters rushing down the gullies that had been barren at the end of the last summer.

For the past few months, White Owl had burrowed into the cave, nursed his broken heart and made a new plan for his future. He had two goals: to travel to this place called Ireland and to get his wife back.

The ride back to the Adair homestead with filled with indecision. He did not want to see her family again, but he knew he had to have more information before he set off for Ireland. Then he would figure out how he was going to get to this foreign land.

Hiding on the ridge above the ranch, White Owl tried to calm his pounding heart. This place held too many memories. His gaze traveled to the barn; remembering their nights of unbridled passion made him ache for his Wild Rose even more.

His long months of solitude had convinced him

of two things: Wild Rose had not left to get away from him, and she had not left here on her own accord. He kept recalling the way she had looked at him up here on this very ridge when she blew him a kiss. He looked over at the exact spot where she had been at that moment and he knew without a doubt he was right. Today he would find out the truth.

He did not have to wait long for his chance. Since it was early morning, Wild Rose's father and twin brother exited the house together and headed for the barn. White Owl knew that they were most likely headed out to ride the range and check on their herd of cattle. Once they were gone, he could make his move. He would get the answers he needed from Wild Rose's mother.

Shortly, the father and son came back out of the barn leading their horses. Although White Owl had hidden Niwaa in a secluded spot among a thick grove of aspens, he was relieved to see that the men were headed in a different direction today. He waited until they were completely out of sight, and just as he was about to start down the slope, the younger brother came out of the house and headed into the barn. He froze in his tracks until the boy was in the barn. He had only taken a couple more steps when the stupid black dog started barking at him.

It was just like old times, he realized. Sneaking down the slope, the dog barking and—wait—no, it was nothing like old times, because his Wild

Rose was not here anymore. Since he was halfway down the slope, he had no choice but to keep going even though the dog continued to bark. He patted his leg in an effort to remind the dog of who he was. "Pepper," he called just loud enough for the dog to hear.

The dog came running toward him with his tail wagging, but not before he had drawn Donavan's attention. The boy came back out of the barn with a rifle in his hand. He spotted White Owl at the same time that the warrior saw him. Donavan immediately raised the gun, but even from a distance, White Owl could see his hands shaking.

"I am not here to cause trouble," White Owl called. He placed his rifle on the ground at his feet. "I just want my wife back," White Owl added.

Donavan remained unmoving, but his terrified expression made him look capable of blowing White Owl's head off at any second.

"Please, Donavan," White Owl pleaded. "Tell me how I can find her. I know she didn't want to leave me, and I have to find her—I have to . . ." His voice trailed off. The dog was now jumping up and down against his thighs trying to get him to pet him, but White Owl did not move as he waited for Donavan's reaction.

The boy's indecision was written on his face. After what seemed like a very long time, Donavan slowly began to lower his gun. "If—if I tell you, will you promise to leave here and never come back?"

White Owl exhaled the breath he had been

holding. "I promise more than that—I promise to never come back, and to love your sister with all of my heart for the rest of my life."

Donavan put the gun down against his thigh and looked up toward the sky for a second before leveling his gaze back on White Owl. "Pa made her leave. She begged and begged to go back with you, but he made her go to my aunt's house in Denver."

White Owl had always believed that there was nothing that could make a warrior cry, but at this moment, he wanted to cry with happiness. His Wild Rose had not run away from him, and he had wasted valuable time with his insecurities and doubts. "Where in Denver?" he finally managed to ask.

"My aunt's house is on the Platte River, next to the schoolhouse. She's the teacher there."

White Owl nodded his head. He remembered Rose telling him about her. "Thank you, Donavan. I will make sure she is well taken care of." He pointed down at his gun, and the boy nodded his head. White Owl carefully bent down, but before grabbing his rifle he patted the pesky dog on top of the head one last time.

Once he had retrieved his gun, he chanced that the boy would not shoot him in the back as he turned away and began walking back toward the hillside. Something moved at the front of the house, and he stopped abruptly. He turned his head slightly and saw Wild Rose's mother standing on the front stoop. They stared at each other briefly and then she raised her hand and waved to him. Her face was filled with sadness, and White Owl realized that she was probably hurting far worse than he was. Because he was going to get his wife back, but she would never get her daughter back. He turned away and began sprinting back up the hill as fast as his legs would carry him.

He had an important date, and she was waiting for him in Denver, along the Platte River. Compared to Ireland, Denver seemed just around the bend.

The trip to Denver was easy for White Owl. He had traveled this route many times, first when he and his brother were young and had been sent to the white man's school to learn their language and customs and many times since then on hunting trips in the surrounding areas.

But never had he felt the euphoria that he experienced on this journey now. Even Niwaa seemed to sense this trip was special, and he galloped tirelessly across the countryside. White Owl traveled only on back trails, and in many places where there were no trails at all. He encountered only an occasional traveler, but he was careful to remain hidden. In no way did he want to delay his arrival in Denver; they had already wasted too much valuable time apart.

When he finally reached the edge of the foothills that surrounded Denver, it was late at night. The pale moonlight afforded him his first glimpse of the settlement in almost fifteen years. White Owl was stunned to see how much the City on the Plains had grown. When he had been here as a child it was barely more than a tent city out in the middle of the vast plains. Then, there had been only a few rows of buildings and houses starting to be erected along the newly built streets. Now, there were so many structures and streets that he was entirely lost. He hoped that he would be able to sneak through the streets unnoticed, but he knew it would be risky even at this time of night.

He tied Niwaa to a large cottonwood close to a small pond. The nearer he had gotten to Denver, the sparser the remnants from the winter snow had become in the higher locations. By the time he was over the low range of mountains and hills that skirted the western side of the city, the snow had completely disappeared from the ground. In this area, the new spring grasses were already abundant, so Niwaa would have plenty to eat and drink until he returned. Although he hoped to find Rose and be back out of the city before morning, he couldn't chance having something happen to his cherished pony.

He removed the black headband from around his head and tucked it into his pack. He twisted his long hair into a tight rope and pulled it up on top of his head. He had an old tan floppy-brimmed hat in his bag that he had taken from a raid on a homestead by Cripple Creek last year, and he arranged the hat down low on his head over his thick hair.

He pulled out his bear coat and put it on over his buckskin outfit. Bears were sacred to his people, so he hoped the coat would bring him luck today. It was his hope that from a distance he would look less like an Indian and more like a trapper or a mountain man, since he knew they were fond of wearing their fur coats year-round to show off their killing skills. But most of all, he hoped that he would be able to reach Wild Rose without encountering anyone who would question him.

Under the cover of darkness, White Owl carefully made his way through the quiet streets. He saw only a couple men from a distance, and they paid him no attention. Finding the Platte River, however, was not as easy. From the time that he had spent here as a child, he vaguely remembered the river. His days back then had been spent learning to read, write, and speak the white man's language or studying their religion and customs. The rich family he had stayed with was more concerned about saving the soul of a heathen and the belief that they would be rewarded in the white man's heaven for this great deed than allowing him to explore the area.

He kept stopping to listen for the sound of running water, but his ears could not detect anything other than the unfamiliar sounds of the city, which for this late hour seemed strange to him. For the remainder of the night, he wandered down the streets and alleys without finding the river. The sun was beginning to peek over the distant horizon when he came upon the river unexpectedly.

He couldn't believe he had not found it sooner, because it cut a wide path right through the middle of the city. The spring runoff from melting snow in the higher mountains had turned the deep waters a dark brown. He paused along its muddy banks and debated which way to go—upstream or downstream? He decided to head down. It felt as though he had already been paddling against the current for the past several months.

The light of the rising sun, however, was making him more than a little nervous. Even with his disguise, he could not chance wandering around in the broad daylight. Before the massacre at the White River Agency, his presence in the city would have drawn mild curiosity, but now, he would probably be shot on the spot. He stayed as close to the river as possible and tried to walk at a leisurely pace so as not to attract too much attention. The houses along the river were similar in size and structure, but it was not until he spotted the little red schoolhouse that he realized his desperate quest was about to come to an end.

Beside the school, in the same fenced area, was a small, white two-story house. The windows were trimmed in the same red paint as the exterior planks of the schoolhouse. White Owl was reminded of Wild Rose's vibrant red hair and its sweet, fresh scent. He was reveling in the idea of those memories soon becoming a reality when the front door of the house suddenly swung open. The only thing that he could do was stand as still as possible and hope that the woman who exited the house would not pay attention to him, because he was standing almost directly in front of the house.

She was another redhead, but her hair was more of a blonde shade than Wild Rose's fiery hue. She was undoubtedly Wild Rose's aunt. The resemblance was striking even from a distance. At this early morning hour, the spring temperature was cold, and the woman pulled her woolen shawl tightly around her shoulders and hurried toward the schoolhouse. Once she was on the front stoop, she took a key out of the pocket of her calico dress and unlocked the door. She disappeared inside the red building.

White Owl waited until the door slammed shut at the schoolhouse before entering the front gate of the white picket fence. He stood at the front door and breathed deep. Rose was so close now that he was overwhelmed by the thought of seeing her again. Gulping hard, he reached up and knocked on the door—softly the first time, then harder a second time.

The door had an oval window of etched glass, but a white lace curtain covered the window. Through the lacy veil, however, he could see her walking toward him. Her hair was loose around her shoulders, the way he loved it. She was wearing a long white nightdress, and a heavy blue knitted shawl was draped around her shoulders. He sucked in his breath.

As she neared the door, her footsteps slowed and then came to a stop. She remained rooted to the spot, staring back at him through the lace of the white curtain. White Owl knew she recognized him, even in his ridiculous outfit.

He could only wait for a few seconds before he had to grab the doorknob . . . thankfully it was not locked. He pushed the door open and looked into those eyes—eyes the color of the summer sky, and the loneliness and heartbreak of the past few months were wiped completely out of his mind.

He stepped over the threshold, but she did not move. Her mouth was open and her eyes wide as if she could not believe he was real. She clutched the shawl in front of her long flowing gown. A smile began to turn up her lips.

"You found me," she said in a voice filled with awe. She stepped a little closer and gazed up into his eyes.

White Owl smiled back. "I was prepared to go to Ireland to find you."

A confused look filtered through her face. "Ireland?" she whispered.

White Owl couldn't stand being this far away any longer. He closed the door behind him and crossed the short distance to where she stood. "They said you went to Ireland because you wanted to get far away from me." He reached out and with a trembling finger touched the side of her smooth cheek. She was not a dream. He saw tears filling the rims her eyes.

"They lied," she said quietly. "I have been counting the days until I could return to you." She touched his face as if she needed reassurance that he was real, too. "Then how did you know to find me here?"

White Owl breathed in the delicious scent of her hair before he answered her. "Donavan," he said.

A poignant smile came over her soft pink lips as she continued to touch his cheek, his nose, his mouth, his chin.

Her touch was like a curing tonic. He felt the hole in his gut beginning to heal. He encircled her waist and pulled her up to him. She did not resist, and the feel of her in his arms made him complete once more. He breathed in the scent of her hair again, and then leaned down to kiss those pink lips. But as his head bent and his eyes closed, he felt a strange presence. His eyes flew open and looked at her face. In anticipation of the kiss, her lids were closed and her mouth pursed and ready. "Wild Rose?"

Her eyes flew open, and her brows drew together quizzically.

White Owl leaned back and looked down at her midsection, where he had just felt the hard little ball that he knew hadn't been there the last time he had seen her. His mouth opened, but no words came out. He looked back up at her face. She was smiling at him as she grabbed one of his hands and placed it on her swollen stomach.

"Your child is excited to meet his father. Feel how he kicks with happiness."

The feel of little thumps against his palm made his legs grow weak, and the awe of realizing that she was carrying his baby was a joy he could not even find the words to describe. He looked at her again. Her radiance illuminated her beautiful face. In the long winter months he had spent alone in the cave at Vermillion Basin dreaming of the day that he would see her again, he had never once imagined that their meeting could be so wondrous.

The realization that she had already been with child when they had been torn apart only increased his hatred of her father. He could only be grateful that they had found each other before the birth of the child, or else White Owl had no doubt that he would have made Paddy Adair regret the day he had ever come between him and his Wild Rose.

"Are you happy about the baby, White Owl?" Rose asked after his long silence. A worried expression had replaced her smile.

"I-I cannot even begin to put my happiness into words. If we had not been together when this child is born—"

Rose placed her finger against his mouth. "But we will be, so let's just remember the love that created this miracle and concentrate on our future."

"The rest of our lives begins today." He placed his hand against her stomach again. A tender grin touched his lips, and he was overcome with emotion again at the realization that he was going to be a father. He pulled his wife close and claimed that much-awaited kiss.

*　*　*

Rose's lips responded to his kiss with an unquenchable thirst; they had been deprived for far too long. She reached up and shoved the floppy hat from his head, releasing his hair from its hold. As the long mass tumbled free she immersed her fingers in its long abundance. She pressed against him with all her strength, fearful that if she let go, he might disappear from her life again.

Much to her dismay, breathing became a necessity, and they were finally forced to part. "I love you, White Owl. And my love grows more with every breath I take."

"And I will love you, my Wild Rose, until I take my dying breath." A teasing smile curved his lips as he pulled back and touched her stomach again, adding, "And I can see how your love for me grows."

Rose felt a blush heat her cheeks. The baby kicked again, and she could see by the way White Owl's eyes widened that he had felt it, too. "Your son is obviously as excited as I am."

White Owl's eyes narrow slightly. "I feel the kick of my daughter, because I can already tell that she is as feisty as her mother."

Rose laughed at his comment. She had not felt this kind of carefree happiness for so long. "I see that we have different opinions about this child. I know without a doubt that it is a boy."

He raised one dark brow up and shook his head. "No, she has the kick of a girl. I know these things."

Rose rolled her eyes and leaned forward again

to revel in his nearness. She laid the side of her face against his broad chest and felt him burrow his face in her hair. Everything was right in their world again . . . or for this moment, at least.

Chapter Twenty-four

"Where are you taking me now?" White Owl asked as Wild Rose pulled him up from the chair he was sitting in. She had already sat him down at the kitchen table and fed him eggs, flapjacks and sausage until he was so stuffed he could barely move. He was glad that he didn't eat white man's food all the time, or he would be as fat as a cow.

He had not been able to take his eyes off her as she moved around the kitchen preparing the morning meal. She had always been the most beautiful woman he had ever seen, but carrying their child had only added to her loveliness. Her brilliant red hair seemed even thicker now as it tumbled down her back in heavy waves, and her face looked smooth and radiant. But it was the small rounded bump in her midsection that kept drawing his attention. There was a tiny child inside of her—his child—and this realization filled him with an equal amount of pride and pain. He could not help worrying about what kind of life he would be able to provide for this child and his wife during such times of turmoil. But he was determined that nothing else would matter as long as they were all together, and he was never letting her out of his sight again.

Wild Rose laughed as they headed down the long hallway past the kitchen. "You look like you need a bath, and my Aunt Maggie has an exceptionally large copper tub."

White Owl remembered the white man's bathtubs from his youth. They had never been as good as bathing in the river, but the thought of the thick muddy waters of the Platte River did not seem very welcoming. Besides, if his Wild Rose was with him, he could make do in a bathtub for one time.

They were in the small washroom now, and he couldn't miss the enormous tub sitting in the center of the room. There was barely enough space to walk around the tub.

"That is a horse's trough, not a tub," he said.

Wild Rose's lyrical laugh rang out again. "My aunt said this was her one big indulgence."

"It is big," White Owl agreed. "Speaking of your aunt, should I be worried about her returning and finding me here?"

"She knows all about you and about my plan to go back to you after the baby was born," Rose explained. "She understands, but she will not be back until lunchtime." She turned loose of his hand and grabbed a water bucket. "I'll start getting the water heated." She glanced at him, adding, "You can get out of those dirty clothes."

White Owl's thoughts were filled with her

words—she had been planning to come back to him. How had he thought for one instant that she had run off to Ireland to get away from him? He told himself that he would never dwell on that thought again as he returned his attention to the present.

Glancing down at himself, White Owl realized he was a sight, and not a good one, at that. The last thing he had been worried about when he was traveling here to find his woman was his clothes. His buckskin shirt and pants were covered with grime and stains, and even his fringed knee-high moccasins were black with mud stains. He was sure his hair and face weren't much cleaner, and he undoubtedly smelled like a horse. No wonder she wanted him to take a bath before she spent too much more time in his presence.

"I'll be getting that water," he said, grabbing the bucket from her. "Where is the water well, or should I get it from the river?" Fleetingly, he thought about being seen if he went to the river to get water, but her next words took care of those worries.

Rose chortled. "Oh, wait till you see this. My aunt has water right here in the house . . . it's the latest modern invention." She led him back into the kitchen to a strange contraption that looked like a long handle attached to a curved pipe. He stared at it quizzically. When she pulled down on the long handle several times and water came gushing out of the curved pipe, White Owl nearly dropped the bucket.

"How is that possible?" he asked as he tried to look up the pipe where the water was pouring out.

"There is a pipe running all the way down to the river from right here in the house," Rose answered with a chuckle. "It is truly amazing!"

White Owl glanced away from the modern wonder and looked at Wild Rose. A frown drew his dark brows together. "Life here is so much easier than it will be with me, you know?"

Her face grew serious and she narrowed her eyes. "The past few months have been the hardest times of my life, White Owl. Don't you ever suggest that I would be better off here, do you hear me?"

The angry expression on her face and her forceful tone convinced White Owl that he should change the subject. "Well, taking a bath in a white man's tub is still not as good as the river."

Wild Rose grinned and her eyes glazed over for a moment. White Owl hoped that she was remembering the baths they shared in the Green River during their wedding trip. His mind was certainly dominated by those passionate memories, and his groin was reminding him of how long it had been since they were together.

"Now, you start hauling that water to the tub and I'll heat some water up to add to it."

White Owl snapped out of his trance and did as he was told. When she ordered him to remove his filthy clothes and step into the deep warm water in the tub, he was glad he had been obedient. The cold waters of the rivers and streams did not even begin to compare to the luxurious feel of this bath. Of course, he didn't admit this to his wife.

As he soaked the trail dust from his body, Rose put his clothes in a washbasin filled with soap and water and began to scrub them against a washboard until they were clean. She took them outside to hang from a line in the backyard.

"Here, let me wash your hair," Rose said as she hurried back to White Owl. She produced a round bar of white soap from a shelf and dunked it into his bathwater. The room filled with the scent that White Owl loved so much. It was the exhilarating smell of her hair, and reminded him of the way the forest smelled after a rainfall. He was helpless to stop the rise of his manhood in the warm water.

Wild Rose was busy scrubbing his scalp with the wonderful-smelling soap and oblivious to his reaction. He tried to ignore the urges that were causing him enormous distress as she began to dump water over his head to rinse the soap out of his hair. The delicious-smelling soap, combined with her nearness, was too much for a man who had been without his woman for so long. When she leaned down to wet the washcloth, White Owl could not control himself.

He grabbed her by the arms with the intention of pulling her down and merely kissing her, but she leaned forward at the same time he pulled her to him, and the next thing he knew, she was lying on top of him in the big tub. The splash of the water went everywhere, and by the time he realized what had happened, the sound of her giggling was also filling the room.

"You could have just asked—I would have climbed in with you," she chuckled.

White Owl could not stop laughing as he looked at the way her wet hair was hanging around her face. Her luminous eyes were shining like a high country lake in the brightest sunshine as her laughter joined with his.

His eyes were drawn lower and he suddenly became serious. Her white cotton gown was nearly transparent and he could see the fullness of her breasts above the roundness of her belly where the fabric clung to her skin and revealed every inch of her blossoming body. He groaned.

"Am I clean enough to make love to you yet?" he asked in a raspy voice. He didn't wait for her answer as he put a hand over one of her breasts, reveling in the fullness that she had not had in the past.

"And here I thought maybe you were worn out from the trip. But now I can feel that you must not be too tired," Rose teased.

White Owl had been far too long without intimacy with his wife to wait any longer. Without hesitation, he began pulling her dripping gown up over her head. She raised her arms to make this task easier. She wore nothing else underneath, so once the gown was out of the way, their wet bodies melded together as White Owl turned her around so that she was facing him and sitting in his lap. He entered her the moment she was settled on top of him; they fit together like a hand in a glove. The months of being alone, dreaming of her, and being afraid of never seeing her again disappeared like a puff of smoke.

They moved together as one—connected by body, heart and soul—as the water splashed up over the sides of the tub. White Owl tried to be gentle, reminding himself of her condition. It was obvious that she was not as limber as she had been before, but he was surprised to discover that even though the feel of her round belly pressed against him, she was as eager and passionate as ever. The idea that she was still so exuberant about making love to him, even as she carried his child, only expanded his own ardor. He moved his hands up to her full breasts as she arched back and cried out in ecstasy. As their love filled every fiber of his body, he made a vow: he would never let anything, or anyone, separate them again.

Chapter Twenty-five

Rose had fantasized about the first time they would make love after their reunion throughout the past few months. But her musing had always envisioned them being together after the birth of their baby. When White Owl had not attempted to make love to her when he first arrived, she had worried that he didn't plan to be intimate with her until after the baby was born. The moment she had been in his arms again, she had yearned to feel him inside of her. Was that normal for a woman in her condition, she wondered?

Now, she realized that she didn't care whether it was normal. She desired her virile husband, and nothing—not even the baby growing within her—could quench that need. With her back to him now, she reclined against him in the tub after their exuberant lovemaking. He tenderly rubbed her swollen belly, and she heard him sigh in contentment. She couldn't imagine feeling any happier. Everything that she had prayed for and dreamed of since her father had torn them apart had just materialized, and months before she had anticipated. She only hoped she was not dreaming this time, but if she was, she never wanted to wake up again.

"I hate to move," White Owl whispered again her ear, "but I think we should be in a more acceptable position before your aunt returns. She might not be so understanding if she walks in on us like this."

As much as Rose hated to admit it, he was right. Besides, her legs were starting to hurt, and her back felt as though it was breaking. Even worse, she was certain she could not raise herself from this awkward position. "I need help. I'm too fat to get up," she admitted in a disgusted tone.

White Owl chuckled, but quickly grew silent when she glanced back over her shoulder and cast him a deadly look of warning. He instantly placed his hands around her expanding waist and helped her to stand up in the tub. He rose with her and carefully lifted her over the side of the deep tub. She grabbed a heavy knit blanket and wrapped it around herself as quickly as possible as she felt a hot fire shoot through her body and settle in her face.

"Why are you acting like that?" White Owl demanded as he stepped over the side of the tub and stood in front of her. "Are you ashamed of my daughter growing in you?"

"No—never!" Rose swallowed hard. "It's just that I look so different now with your son inside of me, that I was afraid—"

"You have never been more beautiful," White Owl said as he reached out to cup her chin with his wet hand. He raised her face up so that they were staring directly into one another's eyes. "As my daughter grows, so will my love and desire for you."

His tenderness made her tremble with happiness, in spite of the fact that he insisted on arguing with her about the sex of the baby. Her love for him encompassed her with such a rush that she felt weak and swooned against him.

"Wild Rose," he yelled as he caught her in his arms. He scooped her up and held her against him as he rushed from the room with her in a blind panic. When he reached the end of the long hall, he looked around until he spotted the settee in the drawing room at the front of the house.

"I'm fine," Rose gasped. He would never want to make love to her again unless she could convince him that it was not unusual for a woman to feel faint when she was with child.

"White Owl," she said firmly as he placed her on the paisley velvet settee and pushed her back against the pillows. "Listen to me, I am fine. Women in my condition get light-headed sometimes." She could tell by his worried expression that he wasn't convinced.

"We harmed my daughter with our lovemaking," he said angrily. He kneeled on the floor beside her, oblivious to the fact that he was naked and dripping wet. His waist-length hair hung over his bare shoulders and was plastered against the sides of his face and down along the bulging muscles of his chest.

Rose rolled her eyes upward and grunted with

aggravation. "Oh, we did not, and it's a son, not a daughter." She couldn't help chuckling when his worry faded into a deep frown and he pouted in a way that made him look like a five-year-old boy. The slamming of the front door interrupted Rose's moment of mirth.

"It's such a beautiful spring day, the children and I are going to have a pic—Oh!" Maggie Carroll stopped dead in her tracks in the doorway of the drawing room.

White Owl shot up from the floor, but then realized his precarious position. He threw his hands over his groin area, but that did little to distract from the situation.

Rose sat up on the settee and exhaled sharply. "Aunt Maggie! What—I mean—oh dear Lord!" She glanced down and realized that the blanket was wadded up around her midsection and her swollen breasts were raised attentively above the blanket. Grabbing the blanket, she yanked it up over her rapidly heaving breasts. Her gaze flitted to White Owl, who was standing in all his naked glory at attention just like her breasts; only he had nothing to cover himself with. She gasped again as her horrified gaze flew to her Aunt Maggie's face.

Maggie had thrown her hands over her eyes in shock. She swung around and presented them with her back. "I-I-I, oh," she choked out. "I'll be-be in the kit-kitchen." She disappeared as she took off running down the hall.

White Owl slowly turned to look down at Rose. His dark skin was a ruddy hue of scarlet, and his hands were still clasped securely over his man parts. Rose could not control the burst of laughter that flew from her mouth. He was supposed to be a feared warrior, yet standing here now, there was nothing fearless about him.

"This is not funny," White Owl growled through gritted teeth. "Your aunt—"

"Will laugh about this someday, too," Rose cut in. She pushed herself up from the settee and wrapped the blanket around herself, tucking the ends in securely above her breasts. "I'll go grab your clothes. I hope they are dry enough."

White Owl huffed. "I don't care if they are soaking wet, you bring them to me now!"

Rose started to smile, but decided against it. He still did not appear to be finding the humor in this yet. "Don't go anywhere while I'm gone," she could not resist adding. If possible, his scowl grew even deeper.

She rushed from the room and headed down the hall, past the doorway to the kitchen and into the washroom. The floor had more water floating on it than was in the tub. She would worry about the mess later. She had a green velvet dressing gown hanging from a hook on the wall, and she quickly slipped it on and tied the long belt around her protruding waist as she entered the kitchen. To get to the backyard and White Owl's freshly washed clothes, she had no choice but to face her aunt.

"Aunt Maggie, I'm so sorry. But it's really not

what you are thinking—I mean—we weren't doing anything there—well, not right then—"

Maggie's hands flew up in the air as she turned toward her niece. Her face was a shade of red that Rose had never seen before, and she shook her head from side to side as she threw her hands over her ears. "No—no. I don't need to know any details. Just get that man of yours some clothes before one of my students decides to come over here to look for me."

"Oh," Rose gasped as she rushed out the back door. They didn't need to traumatize anyone else today, especially one of the students. But most of all, the very last thing they needed right now was for anyone to know that White Owl was here. Hatred of the Utes since the White River Massacre had not diminished, and in fact, was growing worse.

Rose hurried back in with an armload of White Owl's clothes. Her aunt met her at the door with a picnic basket in her hands.

"I will go out this way," Maggie said in a stern voice. "And when I return tonight, I will expect a proper introduction to your husband." She walked past Rose with a toss of her head. Her thick reddish-blonde hair was piled on her head in a loose bun, and her face was still flushed.

Rose gulped, then sighed heavily. She had no doubt her aunt would welcome White Owl with open arms once she had a chance to get to know him—with his clothes on.

He was waiting for her, still as a statue and with his hands frozen in place over his groin. Rose gritted her teeth to keep from laughing again. She held the damp clothes out to him.

"Where is she?" he demanded as he grabbed the clothes and began to slip into his damp suede leggings and loincloth.

"She went back to the school," Rose replied. She finally felt in control of herself, and the urge to giggle had passed, for now.

"Does she want me to leave?"

"No, of course not. She wants a proper introduction when she gets home this evening." Rose helped him pull his suede shirt down over his muscled chest and flat, rippled stomach, triggering a familiar longing. Obviously, she thought again, the child has no effect on my never-ending desire for my husband.

White Owl placed his hands on his narrow hips. "You still think this is funny, don't you?"

Rose shook her head. "Oh no, I-I—" She looked up and saw the glower on his face. It was too much to resist and she couldn't control the peal of laughter that burst forth.

White Owl glared at her for a moment, and then Rose heard him laugh, too. Soon they were holding on to one another shaking with laughter.

"You should've seen yourself," Rose choked out when she finally was able to talk. "A big bad warrior, standing there with your hands holding your-your—" She struggled to find the right description.

"Well, you didn't look any better," White Owl retorted. "Sitting there with your enormous breasts pushed out above the blanket." He stopped when he saw the way her laughing mouth turned into a heavy pout. "I mean, your beautiful, milk-filled, life-giving—"

"You can stop now," she interrupted. "Are they really that enormous?"

His lip curled up on one side as his brow rose up in a distinctive arch. "Yes, and I love them. I hope they stay like that forever, even after my daughter is born."

Chapter Twenty-six

Rose stared at the paper lying on the kitchen table in disbelief.

"I rushed back here as soon as I saw the headlines," Maggie said. "I knew I could not let you leave for the village tonight now." She glanced around. "Where's White Owl?"

Rose drew a shaky breath and said in a distracted voice as she picked up the paper and started to read, "He's taking one last bath. I have a feeling we will have to have a tub in our tepee."

"Well, you can't leave now, Rosie," Maggie repeated just as White Owl entered the room. Her gaze briefly traveled down over his body before settling on his face.

His damp hair was smoothed completely back away from his handsome face, which was scrubbed to a shiny bronzed glow. The suede fringed suit he wore skimmed along his muscled body with just enough snugness to accent every muscle and bulge.

He obviously heard Maggie's words, because he looked back and forth between the two women who were ogling him without shame. "What is going on?" he asked as his gaze settled on Maggie. "What are you talking about?"

Maggie pointed to the paper in Rose's trembling hands.

"Wild Rose?" White Owl approached her tentatively. "What is it?" he asked.

Rose held the paper out, but when she saw the frown on his face, she decided to relate the news to him and pulled the paper back. She remembered he had told her that although he had learned to read as a child, it was difficult for him to decipher written words in the English language now.

"The paper says that all of the Utes from the White River Agency area have been rounded up and taken to a reservation somewhere in Utah." She exhaled sharply and looked up at White Owl, who was staring at the paper as if her words had not sunk in to his mind yet. "I'm so sorry, White Owl. Your family—they all must be at the reservation now."

His jaw clenched. Rose had heard him say many times that he would rather die than live on a white man's reservation. A sick feeling settled in the pit of her stomach.

"I have to finish getting ready for the trip," he said quietly as if he hadn't heard the words Rose had just spoken. He started to turn away.

Maggie stepped close and placed her hand on his arm. "White Owl, you should stay here until after the baby is born. It's not that much longer. Then you and Rose can figure out what you will do next."

White Owl gave her a forced smile. "We will never be able to repay your kindness already, but I have to go back, no matter what is waiting for me."

"Waiting for us," Rose corrected as she placed her hand on his other arm. She sensed she knew what her aunt was thinking, but Rose knew there was nothing either of them could say to convince her to let White Owl leave without her, not after the long separation they had already endured. Nor could she imagine that he would agree to stay here for another couple of months. He had already been confined to the house for the past four days since his surprise arrival. He had tried to hide his restlessness from her, but she knew he was ready to return to the freedom of the life he loved as much as she did. She glanced at the paper, wondering if that life existed anymore.

"Wild Rose," White Owl began just as her thoughts had predicted.

"I will not even let those words come out of your mouth. We have everything ready to go, and we are leaving here together—tonight."

"Soldiers will be looking for renegades to round up to take to the reservation, and I will have to hide like a hunted animal. I can't ask you to do that, especially now." He glanced down at her swollen belly. "I can come back after—"

"Absolutely not!" Rose said. She touched her stomach in a protective manner, and added, "We all leave together, or we all stay here together. There are no other options." She had no doubt that he wanted them to be together just as desperately as she did. She also knew how worried he was for her safety, and now also for their child. Yet she would not allow him to convince himself or her that they would be better off apart.

"We'll leave as soon as the sun sets," he answered in barely more than a whisper. He attempted to smile back at her. The fear in his raven gaze was stronger than the relief in Rose's expression, though.

Leaving her Aunt Maggie was hard, and Rose could not help but shed tears as they rode away from the little white house on the banks of the muddy Platte River. Maggie had gone above and beyond in her duties as an aunt ever since Rose's father had first dumped her on her doorstep all those months ago, and even more so once White Owl had unexpectedly shown up a few days ago.

After her initial shock of finding a naked Indian and her equally naked niece in her drawing room, Maggie had recovered quite quickly and was totally smitten with Rose's dangerously handsome husband. She had asked him endless questions about Indian customs and beliefs and had not shown a moment of discrimination against his people. She said she planned to teach the students in her classroom the things she had learned from him in the hopes that they would develop an understanding of the Indian ways and realize that all people were created the same.

Rose's gratitude had no limits, but she couldn't help laughing inwardly at the shameless way her aunt sometimes flirted with White Owl. It was apparent he had a way of charming all women, and that Rose wasn't the only one to fall under his spell.

Rose was overjoyed, however, that her aunt found him intriguing rather than terrifying. She had no words to thank Maggie for her kindness, and she knew how much it pained her aunt for them to leave tonight. Not only had she and Rose become extremely close during the past few months, but she had been so looking forward to seeing the baby.

In spite of her sorrow over seeing them leave, Maggie had still done everything in her power to help them prepare for the trip back to Milk Creek. In the days preceding their departure, she had purchased a horse from the livery stable for Rose and had ridden out with White Owl to help retrieve Niwaa from the hiding spot where he had left him. Both horses had been kept in her little backyard for the past couple of days, regardless of the fact that she could have gotten in trouble for having the animals on school property. She had gathered necessary supplies for them and was prepared to tell Rose's grandparents yet another story about Rose's cowboy husband showing up unexpectedly and taking her back to Wyoming with him.

Rose glanced back one last time and glimpsed her aunt standing at the kitchen window as they rode along the riverbank. She waved and was certain she had seen her aunt's hand wave back. Another chapter in Rose's life was coming to an end, but she hoped that someday all the hatred and prejudices between the white men and the Indians would finally come to an end, too. Then her family and White Owl's family could all live together in harmony and peace. She just prayed that they would all live long enough to see that day arrive.

Chapter Twenty-seven

The pace they were forced to travel at because of Rose's discomfort in the saddle was agonizingly slow. The same trip that had taken White Owl less than a week when he had journeyed to Denver alone was taking them more than twice as long going back. It was made even longer by the unpredictable Colorado springtime weather.

The first several days and nights had been warm, and the blossoming April countryside had reminded Rose of just how much she had loved it here. She had been in awe of this wilderness ever since she had traveled here with her parents to homestead in the western territory of Colorado nearly three years earlier. There was nothing to compare to the vibrant shades of green grasses and budding aspens. Tiny wildflowers of yellow, blue and purple sprouted everywhere. Their fragrant scent filled the air with a natural perfume.

Then the weather had turned cold, and it had started to rain. They had been forced to hole up in a tiny cave they were fortunate to find along the back trails. The rain had turned to sleet, then snow. The cave became their sanctuary for over a week until the muddy landscape dried out enough for them to resume their journey.

By the time Rose climbed into the saddle again to continue the rest of the way to Milk Creek, her entire body ached so much that she was not sure she would be able to ride much farther. She did not want to complain to White Owl, because he was so anxious to get back to the Milk Creek area to find out more about his tribe's exile. He was certain there would still be some of his tribesmen— maybe even his own family—in the area who had escaped the march to the reservation in Utah. He hoped to meet up with them before the birth of the baby.

As they entered a lush green valley with a deep river running along the base of a pine-covered mountain, an odd sound distracted her from her discomfort.

"What is that?" she asked as she halted her horse and tilted her head to listen. It was a strange chugging sound and reminded her of the steam-ships in the New York harbor when she had lived there as a child.

White Owl stopped Niwaa beside her horse. They were on the top of a small hill overlook-ing the fertile valley. "See that little pool of water down there by the river?"

Rose nodded her head. The water looked like it was flowing out from a protrusion of rocks that clung to the side of the hill on the other side of the river. It tumbled over the craggy rocks like a miniature waterfall and came to settle in a bubbling pool that boiled like a pot over an invisible fire.

"That is called the Steamboat Springs by your people. Years ago it was named that by French trappers. My people call it the Medicine Springs, and we believe it has great healing powers."

"Oh," Rose said excitedly. "It sounds exactly like a steamboat. Is the water hot?"

White Owl shrugged. "It's warm." He scrunched up his face, adding, "And it tastes like rotten eggs, but smells even worse. If the wind blows we will smell it all the way over here."

White Owl's gaze grew distant. "Only a year ago, I visited the Yampah tribe whose village stood in this spot."

The remnants of campfire pits were scattered around the hilltop, and there were several stacks of logs and tepee poles piled throughout the area.

"Where are they?" As soon the words left her mouth, Rose realized the truth. "Oh," she gasped. "They were forced to go to the reservation in Utah."

White Owl nodded but did not speak. He stared out across the valley as if he was remembering the past and mourning the future. Rose drank in the quiet, peaceful beauty of the area. She could only imagine what a wonderful life the Yampah tribe must have had in this incredibly beautiful valley with the abundance of water from the river and the seclusion provided by the surrounding mountains.

"We will stay here tonight," White Owl announced. "But we will need to be careful. There are settlers not far from here. They have lived there for several years, but now that the tribe is gone, we should not alert them to our presence."

"They lived here—in the same area with the Utes?"

White Owl nodded. "Don't sound so surprised, Wild Rose. Not all settlers fight with the Indians."

She clamped her mouth shut as she started to remind him about the kindness her aunt had showed to him. But he was suffering the loss of his people's entire way of life; the last thing he needed right now was for her to make him feel worse. Besides, she had her own needs right now. Her back hurt so bad it was all she could do to swing her leg over the saddle horn. Before she had slid to the ground, White Owl was at her side. He held on to her until he was certain she was steady on her feet.

"You look tired," he said. "We should have stopped sooner."

Rose bent her arms and placed her hands on her lower back and attempted to stretch her weary body. A sharp pain shot through her abdomen, and she quickly straightened up. She glanced at White Owl, but he hadn't noticed her grimace. Moving slowly, she walked over to the clump of purplish chokecherry bushes where he was already spreading out blankets for her to lie down on. He rolled one blanket up so that she could use it for a pillow.

White Owl helped her to the ground, and as she lay back she placed her hands cautiously over her stomach. She was certain their son had grown double his size since they had left Denver. Now, she felt awkward and heavy. Her belly felt as if it was pressing down against her pelvis bone. What if she had miscalculated the impending birth, or what if the baby came early? She had estimated he would be born in late May or early June, but it was only the end of April.

"I'm going down to the river and catch some fish for dinner," White Owl announced after he had cared for the horses.

Rose smiled and waved him on. She was frantic as she waited for another pain to hit, but luckily, nothing happened. She listened to the curious steamboat sound of the bubbling spring. The constant chug, chug, chug never missed a beat. By the time White Owl had returned, the sound had lulled her into a peaceful mood, and she was ravenous. "Did you catch anything?" she called out as he walked toward her.

He snorted indignantly and held up a willow branch with a string of brightly colored rainbow trout hanging from it. "You would doubt it?" he asked in an incredulous voice.

Rose chuckled and shook her head as she pushed herself up to a sitting position. The short rest had done wonders for her aches and pains, and she was feeling so much better.

"I'm cooking tonight," White Owl announced. "You rest."

Rose's eyes widened in surprise. Ute men did not cook, or at least she had never seen one cook in the time she had been with White Owl. But it was an idea she rather liked. Leaning back on the blankets and pillow again, she watched as her husband started a very small fire in one of the abandoned fire pits. He had already cleaned and gutted his catch at the river, so now he took his knife out of its sheath and sharpened several more willows that he had brought from the trees along the riverbank to use as spits to cook the fish on—the willows would not burn immediately when they were placed over the flames, and the fish would be cooked long before the branches got hot enough to catch on fire.

The smell of the fish roasting over the flames made Rose's stomach growl without shame. She pushed herself up from the ground and ambled over to the fire pit to wait for the first fish to be finished cooking.

"I'm starving," she announced as she approached her husband.

He chuckled as he watched her shuffling toward him. "Well, you are eating for yourself and for my daughter, so I am not surprised." He patted the spot next to him on the ground, and helped Rose as she lowered herself down.

She shook her head at his determination that they were having a girl. There was still no doubt in her mind that she was carrying his son.

"You look much better now. Tomorrow we won't ride as far."

Since they were traveling a different route than she had ever been, she had no idea how long they still had to travel, but she hoped it wouldn't be too much farther. The memory of the sharp pain she had felt earlier made her rub nervously at her stomach.

"Is my daughter kicking again?" White Owl placed his palm against the spot she had been rubbing. His face scrunched up. "I don't feel anything."

Rose pushed his hand away. "That's because your son is getting angry at being called a girl by his father."

White Owl chuckled and returned his attention to the fish as Rose watched the sun setting on a nearby mountain to the west. The misty blue sky was painted with shades of pink and orange streaks above and behind the mountain. The longer she stared at the peak, the more she realized that it had a familiar shape.

"Are you staring at the giant mountain?" White Owl asked when he noticed what she was looking at.

"The what?" she chuckled.

White Owl pointed at the mountain. "See, there is the giant's head, and his belly." His finger moved to the south of the mountain as he added, "And there are his legs. He is a sleeping giant."

Rose looked at the mountain from a new perspective and realized that the profile of the mountaintop was an exact replica of a man lying on his back. It truly was a sleeping-giant mountain.

She smiled as she looked back at her husband. "I love it here."

"The Yampah loved it, too," he said sadly. He

held a branch toward her with a sizzling trout on the end of it.

Rose took the branch. "Thank you," she murmured. She wanted to tell him how much she hated her own people right now for what they had done to the Utes, but she couldn't find the right words. His sorrow seemed so deeply rooted that nothing she could say would ease his torment.

As soon as the trout were done cooking, White Owl tossed dirt on the few flames that still sparked in the pit. It was growing dark, and he did not want the fire to be seen by the family that lived down in the valley. As darkness settled over the land, however, Rose noticed the faded lights of the distant house. She crossed her arms over her large belly and wondered about the family who lived there. Had they been sad to see the Yampah go? She guessed her father must be feeling mighty happy right now. He had finally gotten his wish . . . the whites had run the Indians off their own land.

The sharp barking and howling of a pack of coyotes sliced through the silent night. Their yelping was almost like mournful screaming. The chilling sound echoed across the desolate hilltop, making Rose feel that even the coyotes were filled with sorrow to discover that the Utes were gone from here forever.

Chapter Twenty-eight

Rose was sad to leave the valley of the chugging Medicine Springs, the mountain of the sleeping giant and the clear shimmering waters of the Yampah River. She hoped they could return to this beautiful lush valley someday with their first-born son and the other children she was certain they would have in the future.

White Owl lifted her into the saddle and the ache in her back immediately came back. She gritted her teeth. It was going to be a long day. Luckily, White Owl stuck to his plan to stop frequently. Each time she climbed down from the saddle and lay down for a while to rest, hoping the pain would disappear. By the time they stopped for the night, she was becoming optimistic about reaching Milk Creek before their son decided to make an early appearance. White Owl said they should reach the site of his tribe's deserted village by nightfall the next day. Then he would start looking for anyone who might be left in the area. They had no plan beyond that, and Rose couldn't help wondering where they would be when the baby arrived.

After a restless night, Rose woke up to the pain

in her back before she even got in the saddle. She moaned softly as she sat up, and the sound drew White Owl's attention at once. He was at her side before she had a chance to move again.

"What's wrong?" He crouched at her side. "Is it the baby?" His voice was filled with concern and his expression looked to be on the edge of panic.

Rose shook her head. "No, no . . . I'm fine. My body is just getting a bit stiff and sore from all the riding. And your son is becoming a heavy load."

White Owl gave her belly a loving rub. "Once we reach Milk Creek, you can rest while I search for the others. You and I both know of hiding places were the grass is deep and soft." He winked at her.

Rose giggled as she remembered the summer afternoon last year when they had made passionate love in one of the hidden alcoves along Milk Creek. She had no doubt that once she was out of the saddle for a couple of days, she would be just fine. She held her hand up for White Owl to pull her to her feet, since she knew there was no way she would make it up on her own this morning.

With a determination not to give in to her misery, Rose let her husband help her into the saddle again. Since her back was already hurting, the movement of the horse did not seem to be making it any worse as they began the last leg of the trip—for now, anyway. But as the morning wore on, the pain in her back began to radiate around to the front of her abdomen.

"White Owl," she called as he rode in front of

her through a secluded gully where there was no trail to follow. "I think I need to rest for a while."

White Owl pulled up on his reins and jumped down from Niwaa's back before the horse had even come to a complete stop. "What's wrong?" he demanded. They had just stopped barely a mile or so back for her to rest.

Rose shook her head and shrugged. "It's just this stupid pain in my back. It must be from so much riding. I'm sure if I rest for a few more minutes, I'll be fine."

White Owl's worried expression did not fade. He stared up at her for a moment before he reached up and lifted her from the horse's back. He carried her to the shade of a cluster of aspen trees. Rose wrapped her arms around his neck, grateful for his kindness.

"Just give me a minute," she said with a forced smile. "That darn saddle is just so hard and—" She gasped as new type of pain cut through her lower abdomen.

"Wild Rose, the baby is coming now?" His tone was filled with panic.

"No, it's too early, I think."

"You think?" he yelled. "You said early summer."

Rose rolled her eyes upward and shook her head. "That's what I think," she repeated. Last summer and fall, she had been so engrossed in their love affair and then in her new role as his wife that she had not worried about those things. Now, she was not sure when it might have happened.

"What do you want to do?" he asked in a nervous voice. "Should we prepare for the birth?"

"No," she said as she shook her head again. "It's not time. I want to get to Milk Creek. Like you said earlier, I can rest then, and I'll be fine."

He stared at her for a moment with a disconcerting glare. "I don't want to deliver this baby out here, but I don't want anything to happen to you, either." He drew in a heavy breath. "You must promise to tell me if it gets any worse."

Rose forced a smile, "I promise." She wished she felt as confident inwardly as she was attempting to convey to him.

White Owl made Wild Rose ride in front of him so that he could keep a closer eye on her. Every time she even moved slightly in the saddle, his throat felt like it was closing shut and he couldn't breathe. He knew Ute women had babies along the trails to and from their winter and summer homes all the time. But this was his baby . . . and his Wild Rose. The thought of having to deliver their child without the help of his mother or another woman was making him physically sick.

As the day wore on and they stopped constantly for her to rest, White Owl realized they were not going to reach Milk Creek by nightfall. He hated to tell Wild Rose, because the thought of making it back there seemed to be all that kept her going. Since they obviously would not be there until tomorrow he decided that they should just call it a day now, even though it was only late afternoon.

After a good long rest they would reach their destination. One night wouldn't make a difference.

He wondered if Rose realized that they were close to her parents' homestead and that they were probably on Adair land right now. The realization might upset her, since she hated her father and twin brother so much. The one time they had talked about the events that had conspired last fall when her father had forced her to go to Denver, White Owl had also gotten the impression that she was deeply hurt by the fact that her mother hadn't done more to help her. It seemed that she only held Donavan in her heart now, and White Owl felt the same way about the boy. He hoped someday he would have a chance to tell Donavan how grateful he was that he had told him where to find his Wild Rose.

As he rode up beside her to tell her that they were making camp for the night, he realized that she was starting to slump in the saddle. "Wild Rose," he called out in a teasing voice, "are you falling asleep?" But when Niwaa fell in step with her horse, White Owl saw her chin was resting on her chest and her eyes were closed.

"Wild Rose," he shouted, but she didn't respond. His panic stole away his senses for a moment. He yelled her name again and then jumped from Niwaa's back and grabbed the reins of her horse. He grabbed Rose before she could fall and carefully lowered her to the ground. Her head lolled to the side as he shook her and gently tapped the side of her face with his open palm. Her skin felt burning hot. A weak groan escaped from her parted lips. Her lashes fluttered and then her lids parted slightly.

"W-what happened?" she mumbled. She glanced around as if she was disoriented. Her lashes fluttered several more times before she was able to keep her eyes open.

"You fainted, and you have a fever," White Owl said in alarm. She continued to stare up at him as if she didn't understand. White Owl's terror increased. She winced and swallowed hard.

"I think I could have been wrong—the baby might be coming now," she whispered in a weak, frightened voice.

White Owl didn't stop to second-guess himself as he scooped her back up into his arms. He couldn't take any chances with his beloved wife or their child.

Carefully, he lifted her onto Niwaa's back and climbed up behind her. She was as limp as a rag doll. With one hand he grabbed the reins, and then he wrapped his other arm around Wild Rose. She whimpered softly as Niwaa began moving.

The rest of the trip was agonizingly slow. Wild Rose's labor pains were not frequent, and for that, White Owl was more than grateful. But the way she kept drifting in and out of consciousness had him terrified. He didn't think that was normal. On a couple of occasions, he had been nearby when a Ute woman had given birth, and he couldn't remember it being anything like this. He began to berate himself for not listening to her Aunt

Maggie—they should have stayed in Denver until after the birth.

The sun was low on the horizon by the time they reached the ridge above the Adair homestead. The entire area was bathed in a golden glow and did not appear as foreboding as White Owl had remembered. But did Rose's family still love her enough to put aside their hatred for him and help her?

Wild Rose moaned again and gasped as she clutched at her stomach. The pains were getting closer. This terrified White Owl far worse than a bullet from her father's gun. He tightened his hold on her and started down the slope. They had not reached the bottom when the stupid black dog came running toward them, barking ferociously.

"Pepper, good dog," White Owl called, and the dog ceased to bark. But his ruckus had alerted the people in the house. The front door swung open and Paddy Adair came out, rifle in hand. Tate Adair was on his heels with his gun, too. Donavan followed but carried no weapon.

White Owl stopped Niwaa and waited for the men to approach as he called out, "I have Wi—I have Rose, and she needs help."

Paddy Adair continued to walk forward until he was only a couple of yards away, his gaze focused on Rose. After a moment, he looked directly at White Owl. "I don't know how you two ended up together again, but you and your squaw need to get off my property." His voiced dripped with venom as he leveled his rifle at White Owl.

White Owl raised his free hand into the air. "I

will leave, but please, take care of Rose." She was unconscious again in his arms.

Paddy did not back down, and now Tate had moved up to stand beside him with his rifle also aimed at White Owl's head. "You heard my pa," he spat. "You and that-that filthy squaw need to go."

White Owl clenched his teeth in an effort to control his fury. "She might die if she does not get help," he said in a controlled voice. Inwardly, violent tremors shook through his body.

"What's wrong with her?" Donavan called.

"Shut up, boy," Paddy replied without looking back at his youngest son.

White Owl did not answer Donavan's question. If they hated her this much because she was with him, how much more would they despise her once they knew she was having his child? As this tortured thought consumed him, he noticed Rose's mother approaching. She also carried a gun, and he braced himself for another onslaught of hatred.

Colleen Adair marched past her sons and her husband and did not stop until she was directly in front of Niwaa. For one brief instant, as she glanced at her daughter's slumping form, White Owl thought he saw a look of pity. But when she began to raise the shotgun into the air he was consumed with the horror that she was going to shoot him, or worse, her own daughter.

In the next instant, Colleen swung around to face her men. "Paddy, Tate, you drop them guns—now!" Her voice was strong and loud as she pointed the gun at them.

"What in the hell, woman? Have you lost your mind?" Paddy growled. He did not follow her orders to lower his gun. Tate, however, was now holding his gun with the barrel pointed at the ground and his mouth gaping in disbelief.

Colleen tightened her grip on the gun and kept it pointed at her husband. "That's our girl, Paddy. I have hated myself—and you—for the way we treated her. I won't turn my back on her again. I might have lost my mind, Paddy Adair, but I will shoot you if you try to stop me from helping my daughter." She paused and then added, "Or if you try to hurt her husband."

"Colleen, you-you can't be serious?" Paddy blustered. His reddened face was contorted with disbelief. As he stared at his wife, his attention was diverted by his youngest son. Donavan walked past him and took a place at his mother's side.

"If you want to shoot Ma or Rosie and her husband, then you'll have to shoot me, too," he stated in a strong deep voice.

Rose's painful groan intruded on the permeating silence that had settled over the group after Donavan's declaration.

White Owl tightened his grip on her as she writhed in his arms. "Please," he pleaded as he looked at her father.

Colleen's arms grew rigid as she stared down the barrel and wrapped her forefinger around the trigger. "I won't tell you again, drop them guns now!" Her voice was calm and deadly.

Paddy glowered at his wife for a minute longer

before he slowly began to lower the barrel of his gun downward. He glanced back at his oldest son and nodded, but Tate's gun was still dangling toward the ground.

With continued focus on the gun barrel, Colleen said, "Donavan, you go grab them guns."

The boy walked cautiously to his father and brother. He reached out tentatively and clasped on to the butt of his father's rifle. Paddy released his hold on the weapon without resistance. Tate, however, puffed out his chest in an intimidating manner as Donavan reached out to take his gun. He pulled the gun out of Donavan's reach.

"Tate," Colleen warned. "I bet you didn't know I've been practicin' with this gun when you and your pa is out on the range. I think I'm good enough to shoot that gun outta your hand, but I would hate to take that chance. Please, don't make me try."

Tate stared at his mother boldly as if he didn't believe her. He kept the gun held out to his side and refused to give it to his brother.

"Tate!" Paddy Adair growled through gritted teeth. "Do as your ma says."

The older Adair son turned to glare at his father. He growled with defeat and shoved the gun at his younger brother.

"Bring Rose to the house," Colleen ordered without looking away from the barrel of the gun.

White Owl exhaled the breath he had been holding and kicked Niwaa in the sides. As he rode past the Adair men, he kept his eyes focused on the house until he stopped at the front stoop. He slid out of the saddle and then pulled Wild Rose down into his arms. He didn't wait for Colleen or anyone else to catch up with them as he burst through the front door and headed for the curtained doorway that he knew concealed the bedroom that had once belonged to his wife.

He gently placed her on the soft mattress and wiped the stray hairs back from her forehead. Her ghostly white skin was still fiery hot. White Owl's fingers began to shake. A loud gasp from behind him made his entire body flinch.

"S-she's . . ." Colleen's bulging blue eyes stared at Rose's extended belly.

"I think the baby is coming, but she has been unconscious, and now she is burning up." White Owl could see the shock on the woman's face as she continued to focus on the swell of the baby. After what seemed like an eternity, she finally snapped out of her trance.

"Donavan, you boil water." She glanced at White Owl, adding, "You get cold water from the well. Tell Paddy we need some ice from the ice shed."

White Owl jumped out of the way as she shoved past him to get to her daughter. He glanced up at Donavan, who was standing mute in the doorway holding the curtain up with one hand. In his other hand, he still clutched the two rifles. This offered White Owl little assurance because the other two men could have more guns in the house and they might be pointed directly at his head when he walked out of this room. But it was a chance he had to take.

As he followed Donavan out of the room, he was surprised—and relieved—to see the other two men standing in the middle of room without any additional weapons. Paddy met his gaze.

"I heard. I'll get some ice," he said in a resigned voice. He looked at Tate. "You get the water from the well." Tate clenched his fists at his sides as he followed his father out of the room.

White Owl felt cold metal touch his hand. His body tensed. "Wanna hold these while I boil some water?" Donavan asked.

With a numbness overtaking his weary body, White Owl took the weapons. Now that Wild Rose was being taken care of, the colossal realization of what was happening hit him full force. All that they had gone through to be together could come to a screeching halt tonight if she didn't survive the birth of their child.

He placed the guns on the wooden planks of the floor and without another word to Donavan, he walked out of the house. The light was nearly gone as the day was devoured by the night. He walked past Wild Rose's father and twin brother in silence as they both turned to stare at him. His quest took him to the top of the dark ridge; he did not stumble even once. He had traveled this route in the darkness many times last year when he and Wild Rose had met in the hayloft to make love. Now he sat cross-legged at the top of the ridge and stared up at the sky. The *muatagoci*—"new moon"—was the start of a new cycle of life. White Owl held his arms up toward the sliver of the white moon that was rising over the land in the still starless sky and prayed that his Wild Rose would survive this night. There was no doubt in his mind that if she left him, he could not take another breath without her, and his life cycle would end on this night, too.

Chapter Twenty-nine

The misty glow of the dawn blanketed the Colorado landscape. A new day was alive with birds chirping in the distance, an occasional mooing of cattle from the Adairs' herd, and the sound of Niwaa munching on the tender spring grasses that grew along the top of the ridge. The horse had not left his master's side throughout the long night. White Owl watched the animal, thinking of how he had definitely lived up to his name. Niwaa was more than just a pony; he was White's Owl closest friend.

There had not been any activity from the house for several hours, not since someone had retrieved more water from the well sometime during the middle of the night. White Owl waited. He could not go down there until he knew that his wife was well.

Before the sun had finished rising, the door swung open again, and Donavan came charging out. "White Owl!" he yelled. "Where are you? Come now!"

White Owl jumped, but he nearly fell back down to his knees again. He had been sitting on the

ground for so long that his stiff legs did not coop-
erate for a moment. Plus, he could not decipher the
tone of Donavan's voice. The boy sounded like he
was in a panic.

Stumbling and sliding down the slope, White
Owl felt like a hand was squeezing the life out
of his heart. "Is—is she—?" White Owl's voice
cracked as he reached the front of the house.

"Ma wants you," Donavan retorted as he swung
around and went back into the house.

White Owl forced his legs to move forward.
When he entered the house, Paddy and Tate Adair
stood at the far end of the room, and neither of
them spoke. The invisible hand tightened around
White Owl's heart. He stepped toward the heavy
curtain that separated him from his wife. Just as
he reached the threshold, Colleen Adair yanked
the curtain open.

"Well, there you be," she said with a shake of
her head. Her brown hair was hanging around her
face, and she looked exhausted, but she was smiling. "Rose has been asking for you." She stood aside
and motioned for White Owl to enter.

He glimpsed Rose lying in the bed. She was as
pale as the white sheets she lay on, and her eyes
were closed. A blanketed bundle rested in the crook
of her arm. "She's—is she—"

"She'll be fine, now. The fever was raging while
she labored, and I was pretty worried. But the
moment that baby was out, she started to come
around." Colleen patted his arm. "The baby is

small. I think he could be a little early, but he seems to be breathing okay."

"He?" White Owl repeated as he stepped into the room. He inched slowly toward the bed until he was standing over his wife and son. He could not see anything of the child because he was buried so deep in his swaddling, but a little sigh told White Owl that he was in there somewhere. He leaned down to get a closer peek.

"I told you it was a boy," Wild Rose whispered in a weak voice.

White Owl smiled lovingly at her as their eyes met. "I never could deny you anything," he answered. He leaned over and kissed her pale pink lips. She barely had the strength to kiss him back, but she tried, and that was enough for him. His heart was freed from the tight grip, and relief and joy soared through him like an eagle in flight.

"Would you like to hold him?" she whispered.

White Owl nodded as he carefully picked up the soft bundle with his shaking hands. It was so light he wondered if there truly was a baby in there somewhere. But as he began to pull the blanket back, a tiny face with piercing dark eyes stared back up at him. He was taken aback when he realized that such a tiny creature could be looking at him with such an intense gaze. A smile curved his mouth when the miniature person pursed his lips in what appeared to be a pout. Other than his darker skin and hair color, he looked just like his mother, White Owl realized.

"He is . . . so perfect," he said in awe.

"Like his father," Wild Rose said softly.

"And his mother," White Owl added as he sat down on the bed beside her. "What will his name be?"

A tender smile curved Wild Rose's lips. "I want him to have a Ute name."

White Owl drew his thick brows together with a thoughtful expression. "It should be a combination of you and me." He stared at his son; the tiny boy stared back at him intently. "What is a strong Irish name?"

Rose sighed contently as she looked down at their son. "I have always liked the Irish name Conan. It means Little Wolf.

His head rose up and he closed his eyes for a moment, and then nodded. He looked back at his son. "You are Conan Little Wolf." He smiled at Wild Rose, adding, "That sounds like a good Irish-Ute name." The diminutive boy in his arms blinked his dark eyes and sighed again. White Owl was sure that his son had just approved of his new name.

White Owl and Rose stood on the ridge above the Adair homestead. On her back, Rose wore the beautiful leather and wood cradleboard that her husband had made for her to carry their son in while he was small. The top of the carrier was wide and rounded, while the bottom where the baby's feet rested was shaped to a narrow point. White Owl had explained to her that this unique shape was to protect the papoose—the baby—if the cradleboard should fall from a galloping horse. Rose preferred to think of it as just a convenient way to carry her son with her wherever she went.

Conan, now nearly three months old, slept contently in the cozy cradleboard on his mother's back, oblivious to events going on around him.

"See that open area right past the barn there," Paddy Adair pointed out. "That would be a perfect place to build a house."

Colleen squeezed her husband's arm. "They don't want to be that close to us," she chided. She smiled at the younger couple. "And we understand."

Rose giggled as she felt her cheeks grow warm. She definitely did not want to live that close to her parents . . . not with the activities she had planned for as soon as she and her husband were alone again.

But she understood her father's reluctance to have them move too far away, too. Conan had already wrapped every one of them around his teeny little finger, especially his grandfather. With his dark auburn curls, flashing dark eyes and beautiful, golden-hued skin, he was already a little charmer.

"Thank you for your kind offer," White Owl said to Paddy Adair. The two men had come to accept each other once Paddy had finally realized that if he wanted his grandson and his daughter in his life, he would have to change his attitude about the Ute Indians. "But we have to find out about my family. Once we know they are safe, we will decide what to do. Perhaps we will plan on building a house somewhere nearby in the future."

Paddy cleared his throat awkwardly. "We got

plenty of land. You can build miles away and only have to see us every so often, maybe once a week or so." He reached out and gently touched the downy, dark reddish-brown hair on Conan's head. His expression grew soft, as it always did when he looked at his grandson.

White Owl smiled and nodded. "We will talk about that soon. But now we should be on our way."

Rose met his glistening ebony gaze and nodded. She hugged her mother and father one more time and refused to cry, not when she was so happy. She smiled down at them after White Owl had lifted her onto Molly's back, and blew them a kiss as she turned her little mare around and followed her husband down the other side of the slope.

She would not look back, because she knew that they would return soon. But for now, a great adventure awaited her. Her husband rode ahead of her, his waist-length hair billowing out behind him. She kicked Molly in the sides and caught up to him.

White Owl turned to smile at her, and her heart began to beat wildly in her breast. For the rest of her life, she knew she would ride at his side across the vast western lands; their home would be wherever they spread their soft furs . . . and she would continue to pray that their people would all learn to live together in harmony someday.

She thought of the beautiful child sleeping on her back. He was a combination of two opposing worlds, yet already he had built a bridge between them with just his mere existence. Conan Little Wolf was the future, and the handsome Ute warrior, White Owl, who rode at her side, was Rose's life.

CPSIA information can be obtained at www.ICGtesting.com
Printed in the USA
267124BV00004B/3/P